LAWMAN'S LAMENT

When Judge Jonathan B. Lacey is killed in an ambush in Big Springs County, Texas, his dying words to town marshal Dan Marden alter the course of Dan's life. Quitting his work as marshal, Dan embarks upon a hunt for Lacey's murderers, the outlaw Long John Verne and his gang. Then Dan's brother Vance becomes involved in running battles between towns, making Dan's task almost impossible. Now the ex-marshal must struggle to complete his quest.

Books by David Bingley
in the Linford Western Library:

THE BEAUCLERC BRAND
ROGUE'S REMITTANCE
STOLEN STAR
BRIGAND'S BOUNTY
TROUBLESHOOTER ON TRIAL
GREENHORN GORGE
RUSTLERS' MOON
SUNSET SHOWDOWN
TENDERFOOT TRAIL BOSS
HANGTOWN HEIRESS
HELLIONS' HIDEAWAY
THE JUDGE'S TERRITORY
KILLERS' CANYON
SIX-SHOOTER JUNCTION
THE DIAMOND KID
RED ROCK RENEGADES
HELLIONS AT LARGE
BUZZARD'S BREED
REDMAN RANGE

DAVID BINGLEY

LAWMAN'S LAMENT

Complete and Unabridged

LINFORD
Leicester

First published in Great Britain in 1973

First Linford Edition
published 2007

British Library CIP Data

Bingley, David
    Lawman's lament.—Large print ed.—
Linford western library
    1. Western stories
    2. Large type books
    I. Title
    823.9′14 [F]

ISBN 978–1–84617–584–8

Published by
F. A. Thorpe (Publishing)
Anstey, Leicestershire

Set by Words & Graphics Ltd.
Anstey, Leicestershire
Printed and bound in Great Britain by
T. J. International Ltd., Padstow, Cornwall

This book is printed on acid-free paper

1

Not many people were using the regular trail which meandered north-westwards out of Redrock at one o'clock in the afternoon. The brassy, dehydrating sun of early summer was responsible for that. In fact, the whole of Big Springs County, situated towards the northern boundaries of East Texas, was baking in the oppressive heat which threatened to dry out the lesser rivers and creeks of the region.

Town Marshal Dan Marden, mounted on a big-boned dun horse with a black mane and tail, stared down at the eroded undulating track from time to time, trying to read recent sign merely to occupy his mind.

Marden was a lean, muscular fellow who looked rather more mature than his twenty-five years. Short, curling auburn brows and neat, tapering

1

sideburns like copper wire broke up the contours of his thin face, which was at that time set in a thoughtful expression. His wide, mobile mouth was still. Premature crowsfeet wrinkles came and went at the outer ends of his brown penetrating eyes as he blinked.

From time to time he sniffed on trail dust and massaged his long nose without being aware of it. He had on a dark blue shirt, a bandanna of a lighter shade and a swinging black leather vest. A broad-brimmed, narrow-crowned, dented black Stetson shaded his eyes and concealed a good head of hair trimmed fairly short on top.

His first term of office as town marshal of Redrock had almost run its course. In the early days there had been one or two tricky moments when visiting riders with notched gun butts had tested out his youthful authority. Dan would have been the first to admit that he had been lucky in his hostile encounters. Each time he had managed to come out on top, and the confidence which the townsfolk had placed in him had been vindicated.

Never before in the comparatively short history of the town had a marshal so young been appointed. He knew that the opportunity had come his way solely because of the esteem which mature townsmen felt for his father, a local doctor who had joined the Confederate forces during the war between the North and South, and who had been killed in the latter days of the struggle.

Doctor Sam Marden's widow had survived her husband for several years. At this time, when Dan was making his official ride and brooding over his past and future, his mother had been dead for five years. Dan and his younger brother, Vance, were the last of the Mardens in that area.

The distant staccato knocking of a woodpecker restored horse and rider to some semblance of alertness. Dan pushed thoughts of his family and future into the background and concentrated again upon his present self-imposed assignment.

The number of times when he had ridden clear of the town boundaries on official business had been few and far between. On this occasion, he was riding out to meet and escort one Jonathan B. Lacey, a circuit judge who had his home on the outskirts of town.

Temporarily secured in the cells of Redrock's peace office were three known outlaws, members of a notorious gang led by Long John Verne and his formidable half-brothers. Bronc Malloy, Dan's deputy, had been fortunate enough to come upon the prisoners, Rod and Slim Ferris and Jonas McGall, when they were stupefied with liquor after robbing a homesteader on the outskirts of town.

Bronc, a fairly efficient peace officer without much talent, probably hoped that his capture of the outlaws might put him in the running for Dan's job when they had to be re-elected in a few days' time.

The capture of the trio had caused a stir throughout the county. It had also caused trouble for the authorities because Long John Verne was a man who looked after his own, and he had sworn to have them out of cells before sentence could be passed upon them prior to their removal to the penitentiary.

In ordinary circumstances, the outlaws would have been transferred to Middleton, once called Middletown, for trial, but because of the risks involved in transferring them, it had been arranged that Judge Lacey should officiate in Redrock. The judge was one of the most respected citizens of Redrock and a useful friend to the Marden boys.

On account of the threats rumoured to have been issued by Long John Verne, Dan had taken it upon himself to leave the town which depended upon him and ride to meet the judge, who was on his way, unescorted, from the town of Ford City, well to the north-west.

For a marshal hoping to achieve re-election, this move might have been ill-conceived, but Dan would rather have seen another get his job than leave the judge unprotected in his time of need.

The long, powerful stride of the dun was bringing them steadily nearer to the southern extremity of Coyote Ridge, a lengthy wooded sprawl of rock hogsback which extended for nearly two miles in a north — south direction. It was along the eastern perimeter of the ridge that the youthful marshal hoped to meet the judge.

As the southern extremity of the ridge began to bulk upwards on his left, Dan groped around for his spyglass, determined to give the half-hidden track ahead of him a close scrutiny. Here and there, he spotted birds of many varieties. A sudden movement as he panned the glass betrayed the agility of a red squirrel, springing with great concentration from bough to bough and tree to tree.

Of the judge's buckboard, however, there was no sign. The visible parts of the trail ahead appeared to be deserted as far as humans were concerned. High above the ridge, near the part where the narrow central pass was masked by dwarf pines, a solitary turkey buzzard flapped across the sky on lazy wings.

Dan watched it for a moment and then collapsed his glass. He had not made much mention of his fears for the judge's safety in town. Both he and his brother had plenty of imagination, and he hoped that his fears were unfounded. Judge Lacey's reputation for fairness and incorruptibility was well known throughout most of Texas, but his reputation would not protect him if the Verne boys decided to delay the trial of their partners by interfering with him.

On a previous occasion, Dan had remonstrated with the judge for not having at least one armed man along with him between towns, but the old lawyer had rebuked him for being too keen in his job and had continued to do most of his journeyings alone.

The judge's eyes were still good, and in his younger days he had often used his revolver to maintain order in the face of threats from the body of his court. Given a fair chance, he could still give a good account of himself, but whoever heard of a bunch of outlaw ambushers giving an old man a fair chance in the middle of nowhere? The lawful presided in court, but the lawless held sway, more often than not, in the wilderness.

Dan yawned. His neck was beginning to prickle with perspiration, a sure sign that he was unsettled. Moreover, the dun was showing by its action that it was in need of a rest. He had an indescribable feeling that something was about to happen. As a result, his breathing became more shallow. He was holding himself in, using his sense to the utmost, waiting for trouble.

His questing brown eyes looked for the unusual, for something outside the pattern provided by nature. He scanned the upper reaches of the ridge, noting the niches where the birds would be nesting, picking out the heat-hazed rock from the thick foliage which camou-flaged it.

Where, he wondered, would ambushers hide themselves on a rocky eminence such as Coyote Ridge, if they wanted to gun down a man approaching from the north on a buckboard? Dan came to the conclusion that he was not thinking properly. Experienced ambushers would not climb high. They might send one of their number to a high spot from which to observe, but the guns which were going to do the damage would be hidden among the trailside rocks at the lower level.

Such thoughts led to his own position. If he happened to blunder upon an ambush spot before the intended victim he might run grave risks himself. After all, a man alone on horseback was every bit as easy a target to practised gunmen as was a loner on a buckboard. And the star pinned to his vest might be an added attraction!

The sounds which Dan dreaded were long in coming. But come they did, and as soon as he was sure that they were muted reverberating gunshots, he was thrown into a quandary. He had traversed almost three-quarters of the length of the great rock barrier and his straining ears told him that the shots were being fired on the other side of it. What was he to do?

After all, he had nothing at all to confirm that the shots were fired at his friend, the judge. Moreover, there was the problem of deciding which way to go to investigate. Should he keep on riding to the northern tip of the ridge and then backtrack down the other side? Or should he turn around in his tracks and attempt to help by negotiating the pass over the central heights?

Another flurry of shots echoed tantalisingly towards him, telling him that whatever was happening was still developing. He reined in and clamped his legs hard around the dun's barrel, gripped by indecision. After a brief spell of hesitancy, during which he decided to assume that his friend was in danger, he felt sure that the second fusillade had come from a location slightly further south than the first.

Suddenly, there swam into his mind's eye a vision of a running battle. A buckboard hotly pursued by following riders bent upon murder. If the judge had deliberately detoured around the other side of the ridge and he was travelling south, then it would be foolhardy of Dan to keep on riding up the east side. If his judgement was right, the situation called for a swift change around and a breakneck climb and thrust over the central pass.

He turned the dun as he came to a decision, talking sharply to it in a tone he used only when he was in some sort of trouble. The animal responded well and they began to make ground in the reverse direction. The beast lengthened its stride. Its long black tail stretched out behind it. The dust began to fly from under the pounding hooves.

On the move, Dan found it harder to interpret the muted sounds of gunfire, but he was sure that he had made the right decision in turning about. His mind began to work on other calculations.

Two well-bred and evenly matched horses in the shafts of a buckboard were capable of putting up a fine performance, but when they had covered several miles already their stamina would be sapped. He wondered how long it would take for a handful of determined riders on fresh horses to overtake a vehicle like the judge's.

Not very long, and that was for sure. In the meantime, there was the zigzag climbing path to be negotiated, then the pass, and finally the precipitous descent on the other side, rendered no doubt more hazardous by flying bullets.

Dan found the bottom of the track and turned the reluctant dun's head towards it. As the animal slowly negotiated the narrow winding path, the tensed rider felt a tiring of another set of muscles as he leaned forward and braced himself to assist in the climb.

About two-thirds of the way up, the dun definitely began to flag. Dan was in sympathy with it, but he knew that a man's life might depend upon the effort they put into the next few minutes. He slapped the steaming rump and encouraged it still further.

The shots which echoed through the pass a minute later seemed to suggest that the pursued and pursuers had ceased to move south, but Dan could not be sure. He was breathing through his mouth and studying the twin streamers coming from his horse's nostrils as he pondered again. If progress had stopped, it meant that the judge or whoever it was had gone to earth and that his attackers were encroaching upon his position.

Dan found himself fervently hoping that he had misread the events on the other side of the ridge. The pass was still some little distance away. It would take time to reach it. Even when he managed to get that far, the trail on the other side was too far away for accurate shooting against men dug in.

Twenty yards from the top, he dismounted, fearful about the strain he had put upon his mount. Walking at the head, he finally moved into the narrow pass. Perspiration glued his hatband to his head and then started to trickle down his brow and into his sideburns.

He knew then that the judge meant a lot to him. It was not just that he might some day become Vance's father-in-law. Dan had for the old man both respect and affection. Ten yards clear on the other side, he halted the heaving dun and brushed salt perspiration from his forehead before extending his glass and putting it to his right eye.

The first thing he learned was that the buckboard had gone off the trail; probably capsized when a wheel hit a rock while the vehicle was travelling at speed. There was no gun firing from any place near to where the panting pair of grey shaft horses nervously shifted their feet in the long grass wide of the trail.

Three hostile guns, all shoulder weapons, were firing at fairly regular intervals from either side of the trail. Dan studied the bobbing head and shoulders of the gunman far below him on the near side. The sight of the advancing killer heightened his resolve. He had already identified the matched horses attached to the overturned vehicle. He knew that the judge, dead or alive was somewhere near them hidden amid the trees and stunted bushes.

He gave the dun the speediest wipe-down with bunch grass which it had ever had, and hauled his Winchester out of the scabbard.

2

For nearly a minute, he paused with the treasured shoulder weapon held to his body. Then, when he was beginning to think that the shooting was finished, that he was too late, the attacking guns blazed again. It was difficult to pinpoint the source of all the shots as the three marksmen were widely separated, but Dan made the effort.

His first two shells were aimed at the dense scrub on the far side of the trail. While he was startling the men hiding there, and filling the area with new gun noises, the man on the near side hurriedly shifted his position. Dan, however, sent a shot after him which ricocheted very close and made the third man cower back against a rock in sudden panic.

Once again, the intruder had to assume the worst. Not that the judge was eliminated, but that he was in imminent danger. Bearing this possibility in mind, Dan leapt for his saddle, coaxed the dun forward and headed the animal on the first of the downgrade on the west side.

The track zigzagged backwards and forwards over perhaps four hundred feet. In places it had ceased to be a track because of light falls of soil and the displacement of boulders. Horse and man had their work cut out to stay on the track without any further complications.

After their initial shock, the hostile guns down below began to fire back. For a time, they harassed the descending rider, although their bullets did him little harm other than to get on his nerves. While he was on the high ground, bushes and shrubs screened him very efficiently from anyone directly at the foot of the ridge.

Although he was watching the track and studying how the dun was progressing, Dan had his ears working for him. He wanted to know, above all, whether there was any response from the region he supposed the judge to be in. For a time, the ambushers appeared to take it in turn to fire up at him, but at no time was he aware of a fourth rifle.

Judge Lacey, he felt sure, carried a shoulder weapon with him on his travels between towns. If only Dan could hear something to reassure him . . .

At a turn in the trail some five minutes later, two rifles, the ones firing from the far side of the trail, pumped a series of accurate bullets up at him. One passed under the belly of the dun and a second tweaked the brim of Dan's Stetson.

The surprise was sufficient to make him crouch down upon the fore part of his saddle and think again about the distance between him and his enemies. Soon, he would be in a dangerous situation, unless he could panic them into making some sort of a move before he came too near.

He felt his anger mounting as he strove to get nearer to the potential victim he had come to protect. A fall of soil half way along another stretch almost precipitated a crisis. The dun pulled up, whinnying with fright, and Dan had to dismount to prevent it from making a false step which would plunge them down the hillside.

Sensing his predicament, although they could not clearly see him, two of the marksmen began to probe his position. The bark of the third rifle close below him made him think that he could do something to stir things up for the opposition.

He leaned backwards against the slope and deliberately pushed loose soil further down. Some small stones followed. He paused in his labours and picked out one or two, which he began to hurl away from him in the direction of the third gun. Next, he backtracked about five yards before firing a couple of angry shots across the track.

Altogether, the action had not lasted very long, but the troubled young peace officer had a brooding feeling that every minute delayed was a setback. This unshakable feeling moved him to further and risky action. He hauled back the dun, mounted up hastily and urged it to negotiate the spot where the fall had taken place. The obstacle called for a short leap of between four and five feet.

For a second or more, Dan felt that it might refuse, and yet he had trained it well, having had a good deal of practice in horse-handling during his cow-punching days on the west coast. He used his rowels and that sudden assault upon the animal's flanks had the desired effect. It sailed into the air, cleared the area of the fall by two feet and confirmed its precarious balance on landing.

This mild success boosted Dan's confidence. Leaving the forward progress to the quadruped, he pulled his six-gun and pumped four or five shells into the rocks where the nearest ambusher was hiding. The effect of this move was startling. The man at the receiving end yelled harshly as the bullets whizzed round him.

Dan was looking elsewhere when the fellow broke cover. For an instant he was revealed, dancing from one prominent rock to another, and then he was out of sight again and still heading for the trail a few yards farther north.

Nearing another turn in the precipitous path, Dan heard the first promising clatter of harness. He hoped it meant what he thought: that the attackers were rather belatedly making a move to depart. Suddenly alerted by this new hope, he turned in the saddle and stared at the foliage beyond the trail.

Again came the sounds of saddle horses on the move, but he saw nothing at that time and, for his pains, he lost his balance along with the dun and only just succeeded in getting both boots out of the stirrups before the calamitous fall began.

Suddenly the earth was spinning. Everything was jolting rock and tearing prickly thorn. Ferns brushed his face and earth gave way beneath him. His shoulder weapon slipped from the scabbard, bounced on a rock and discharged itself. Fortunately, neither horse nor rider were in the line of fire.

Two flailing hooves narrowly missed the man as the horse rolled untidily past him. Their paths diverged, although they were both rapidly losing altitude. No one fired at them. Within seconds, they had been brought up short by trailside rocks. The horse somersaulted through them. It lay on its side for upwards of a minute, raising its neck in a dazed fashion.

Dan Marden landed between the two upper surfaces of a pair of rocks, his breath temporarily knocked out of him. He blinked hard, minus his hat. His senses were swimming and he fought to get them under control. The barrel of his .45 Colt, still clutched in his right hand, circled in front of his face.

He murmured: 'Judge, I sure do hope you're doin' better than I am.'

His rib cage was bruised through violent contact with the rocks. While he panted for breath, rifles started to fire again. In his depleted state, he found himself wondering whether they were aiming at him or the judge. Sounds of men mounting followed and finally horses' shod hooves rung on eroded rocks of the trail itself.

And still Dan's head was not quite clear. He wondered if they were coming his way or going the other. As the sounds faded, he shook his head rather carefully. His ears were working properly. The horsemen really were retreating — going away from him.

He began to feel frustrated, having secured the withdrawal. Making an effort, he staggered and fell over the last of the trailside rock into the open. The third of the riders showed uptrail a piece, just emerging for his getaway.

Dan clenched his teeth. He brought

up the gun and fired after the runaway. Unfortunately, his aim was out and his balance was still far from good. He had stumbled rather fortunately when the retreating ambusher fired two parting shots at him.

The ensuing silence seemed unnatural. Some three minutes had elapsed before the discomfited peace officer had recovered sufficiently to go in search of the judge.

* * *

Jonathan B. Lacey, for once, looked his sixty years.

He had dragged himself clear of the trailside rocks and propped his back against a leaning tree bole. He was slowly blinking the steel-grey eyes which had so shaken malefactors in the past in court. His rifle was clutched in his right hand, but he did not seem to have the required strength to line it up on anyone who approached him.

Dan came to a halt five yards away

from him, breathing heavily and not feeling any marked sense of relief now that he knew his friend was still alive. The judge looked far gone. A spreading patch of blood stained his white shirt front on the left side. A bullet had penetrated his back and played havoc with his chest.

He was hatless. His long white hair was awry. His hollow cheeks seemed more eroded than ever. He had the look of a man who had almost finished his time on earth. A twig snapped under Dan's feet. The grey eyes were screwed tightly shut and then blinked open. The hand on the rifle tightened its grip.

'It's me, Judge, Dan Marden. Jest take it easy. The trouble is over now. Your ambushers have retreated.'

Dan stepped closer, putting down his revolver and kneeling beside the fallen man. He knew at once that the veteran lawyer was dying. He had not been present at many occasions like this. He felt that a woman's presence might have been more fitting, and his thoughts turned briefly towards Della, the judge's daughter. How would she take this tragic loss?

'It sure is a pity you didn't happen along a while sooner, Dan, but you couldn't have known I'd turn off the regular trail, so I guess you did well to get here at all before I finally ran out of time.'

'I sure am sorry, Judge. The Verne brothers must have done this, but believe me they'll suffer for it. Hold on a minute, I'll go and get a canteen of water.'

The judge smiled bleakly, but shook his head. 'There's no time for that, son. Stay close an' give heed to what I have to say. Come to think of it, there ain't many men I'd want to have by me at a time like this.'

Dan judged the last comment to be a compliment. He sighed, and stayed close.

'Dan, one of these days the law in the West will be strong enough to prevent happenings like this one from takin' place. Till then, young determined fellows such as yourself will have to fight on.'

The older man winced as a pain spread in his chest. Dan waited and wondered how much longer the judge would stay coherent.

'I think you were right about the outlaws. I feel sure they were the Verne boys. But I'm also sure that you an' I, the law enforcers, have an enemy back there in Redrock. I want you to do what you can about the Vernes. I also want my daughter protected.'

The dying man bit hard on his underlip, closing his eyes and fighting hard with the creeping inertia of death.

'Then there's your brother, Vance. He — '

At this juncture, the old man choked on his words. A tiny trickle of blood escaped from the corner of his mouth. His expression changed to one of sudden bleakness. His nostrils flared, making his aquiline nose seem sharper than ever. It was rather disconcerting for the onlooker. For a few seconds Dan wondered if Vance had seriously displeased the judge in any way, but that was scarcely possible seeing as how Vance and Della, the judge's daughter, had an understanding about the future. Dan put down the change of expression to the intensity of pain.

A few seconds later, the old man died, gripping Dan's right hand with his free one. The handsome old head circled once, rather loosely on the lean neck, and then settled with the face hidden. Dan carefully tilted back the head and made sure that the eyes were closed. He then stood up, squared his shoulders and slowly walked away to collect their respective belongings.

3

Earlier that day, the long white cloth streamer which bore the word 'Welcome' between two high buildings at the west end of Redrock had been washed and rehung. Nevertheless, as Dan Marden drove the two-horse buckboard underneath it towards five in the early evening, it appeared to be rather faded.

Here and there, loafers moved away from the benches and walls and closely examined the vehicle which they knew to be the property of Judge Lacey. It did not require much intelligence to read the signs. The town marshal was up on the box, alone. His riding horse was attached to the rear, and there was an ominous blanketed bundle stretched along the boards and under the seat.

Dan was aware of many startled eye

glances. His expression precluded conversation. Those who wanted to know more moved along the sidewalks, following the conveyance towards the peace office which was almost halfway along the main street.

Avoiding a group of three hitched riding horses outside the building next door, Dan steered the shaft horses towards the rail, braked and jumped down. As he did so, two men who had been seated on a bench outside rose to meet him. They were an ill-assorted couple.

One was Shamus Rent, a lean, stooping character in his middle sixties, who acted as a general handyman about town and part-time jailer to the office. Shamus sucked in his lips over toothless gums and massaged his flowing white beard.

'Did you have trouble, Dan?' he asked in a piping voice.

Dan nodded. He hesitated in front of the pair, as though he was not quite sure how much information to divulge straight away. The other man was a visiting lawyer, James H. Blane, from Middleton, the county seat. Blane was the lawyer engaged to defend the trio of outlaws captured by the deputy, Bronc Malloy. Obviously, he would have to be told something of what had happened.

Blane was a bluff, thick-set fifty-year-old. His piercing bulbous grey eyes and heavy brown moustache were widely known in the courtrooms of northern Texas. He waited, shifting his weight from one foot to the other and adjusting the large black curly-brimmed hat which hid his formidable quiff of hair. His frockcoat made him look more barrel-chested than he really was.

'Well, Marshal? Shouldn't we know the worst?'

'Judge Lacey has met with a fatal accident. He was ambushed on the other side of Coyote Ridge before I got near enough to protect him. If you could go along to the offices of Hector March, Mr Blane, I'll be along there as soon as I've been to the Lacey house. I have to break the news to his kin.'

Blane appeared to hesitate, but he made up his mind and nodded vigorously. 'All right, Marshal, I'll wait for you there. Maybe I ought to call the doctor and the undertaker. Would that help?'

Dan thanked him and said that he would be obliged. He then pushed the jailer before him into the office, where he found Bronc Malloy sitting at his desk reading a paper with a pair of six-guns readily to hand before him.

Malloy was a sallow-skinned man in his middle thirties with high cheek-bones and a thin black moustache which accentuated his turned-down mouth. He wrinkled his brow, slightly shifting the position of his stained, flat-crowned grey Stetson, and stuck his thumbs in the armholes of his grey cloth vest. There was no warmth in his manner as he spoke.

'You took a long time, Dan. I was beginnin' to wonder if everything was all right.'

'Judge Lacey has been eliminated, Bronc. I want you to leave Shamus in charge here for a few minutes, so that you can come along to the Lacey house with me. Jest leave everything, will you? I won't keep you long.'

Malloy stared hard at the rear corridor, down which were the cells which contained the three outlaws. He seemed reluctant to come away from the building which housed them. As Dan started back from the door, he suddenly stood up, collected his shooting irons and followed him to the door.

Dan pushed his way through a small crowd and leapt on to the box. Bronc joined him and they drove off. By gestures, the marshal managed to disperse many of the would-be sightseers who wanted to follow him to the Lacey house.

He breathed more easily when they faded away at the next intersection. Rapidly, he outlined the situation as he had known it around Coyote Ridge. Surprise and other emotions chased themselves across the deputy's sallow face. Dan, who knew all about his ambitions, was brusque with him.

On the northern outskirts of town he steered towards the white low fence which surrounded the judge's residence. Mary Forgan, a neat, plump little grey-haired woman in her middle fifties, who was Lacey's sister-in-law, and who kept house for him and his daughter since Mrs Lacey had died some years previously, rose from a swinging garden seat beside the house and came to meet them.

Dan jumped to the ground, surveyed the front of the house to see if young Della was about. He took off his hat and stooped close to Miss Forgan, hoping that he could find words to soften the blow she was about to receive.

'It's bad news, isn't it, Dan? I can tell by your face.'

'Yes, indeed, Miss Forgan. He wasn't on the route I expected, and he had received a fatal wound before I got to him. Is there some place we can move him for you? My deputy is here to help me.'

Mary Forgan dabbed away premature tears, drew herself up to her full height and took in a deep breath. 'In the back parlour will be the best place, I think, if you'll be so kind. I'll open the doors for you.'

Carefully, they slid the blanket-wrapped bundle out and over the tailboard of the vehicle, and Dan took the head. He backed in through the gate and up the steps, with Bronc following him, bringing up the legs and juggling with his hat.

They negotiated the front door and the hall and were going through to the rear of the house when Della Lacey danced out of her bedroom on the upper floor and came racing down the steps, thinking that she was about to greet her father.

Dan glanced up at her, but kept on moving.

'Howdy, Dan?' the girl called. She

slowed to a stop, halfway down, breathing hard, in a peasant-style white blouse and a short grey riding skirt. Her long blonde hair was parted high and held back at the sides by clips. Her green eyes rounded with shock. She pursed her full lips and then all the vim and vigour seemed to drain from her lightly sunburnt face.

'What is it?' she queried in a hoarse whisper. 'It can't be father, can it? What's happened?'

Her voice went off-key. She completed the journey down the stairs and was met in the doorway to the back parlour by her aunt, who firmly held her back and imposed a kind of matronly discipline upon her.

While the men were manoeuvring the body on to the long settee, the aunt did what she could to control the difficult situation.

'Your Pa always said that when calamity struck us, we had to act like real adults and keep a stiff upper lip in public. He's no longer with us, darlin', an' you've got to face up to the shock. Come an' sit down. I'll get you a drink of something.'

Mary steered the girl into a padded winged chair and hurried out of the room in search of the brandy bottle. Slowly, the girl, who was no more than twenty, came out of her shock. Colour returned to her face in excess of normal.

'What happened, Marshal Marden?'

Her voice sounded hostile, distant and accusing. She stood poised in a corner, near a window, and it was clear that she intended to have answers to her questions and that she was fully out of sympathy with Dan. The latter murmured a quiet instruction to Malloy, who withdrew slowly to attend to the shaft horses, the buckboard and the tired dun attached to the tailboard.

Malloy's calculating expression showed that he was intrigued by Della's impending attack upon his senior. He was slow to clear the door of the back parlour and as he did so, he turned and looked back, his eyes full of speculation. Mary Forgan noticed his interest and her pale face mirrored displeasure.

'All right, Dan, so your subordinate has gone. Now will you tell me the details of my father's death, or do I have to wait for a coroner's report or something of the sort?'

'Della, don't speak to Dan in that tone of voice,' Mary protested sharply. 'He's been under a strain for a very long time. Here, take this brandy, an' don't speak again until you have drunk it. Dan, I'd be obliged if you'd take a seat and ignore my niece's tone of voice. I'm sure you're much more understandin' than she is.'

For a few seconds, Mary's request was wasted upon Dan, but he blinked himself out of his state of shock and retreated to an upright chair on which he gingerly lowered his weight. In spite of his protest, a small glass of brandy was placed in his hand. With Mary seated midway between them, the exchanges were put off for a time.

Dan finished his liquor first, and felt some relief due to the way in which it coursed through his body. Della drank inexpertly, and almost needed a pat on the back to check the cough which the fiery liquid gave her. The girl declined her aunt's help, and finished the stimulant with what dignity she could muster.

Dan did not wait to be asked again. 'Della, your father was attacked on the far side of Coyote Ridge by three gunmen, members of the Verne gang, men who had sworn to kill him. Using his initiative, the judge took the westerly route in an effort to throw off his pursuers.

'Unfortunately, they overtook him and the odds against him were too great. I shall regret all my life arrivin' too late to put off the inevitable.'

Dan's troubled eyes strayed away from the girl's pent-up face to that of the older woman, who nodded in sympathy. There was an uneasy silence in the room for several seconds. The girl broke it by laughing without humour in an off-key voice.

'So, the older of the two capable Marden brothers, the one who always seemed to be so grown up, the town marshal, no less, has fallen down in his self-imposed task to help a man who was probably his most influential friend.'

'Della, that's enough!' the aunt protested again.

'He worked it all out beautifully, how the judge would be in danger from his enemies, and then he took off. Only he allowed the outlaws to get to their victim first! Sometimes I wonder if Vance, your brother, isn't really far more grown up. I can't think that he would have made such a costly mistake as this one.'

'Think what you like about Vance an' me,' Dan replied angrily, 'but you might at least try to keep a sense of proportion. Nearing death your father sounded much more reasonable than his spoiled daughter!'

Dan had risen to his feet, toying with his hat. He regretted his angry retort as soon as the words were out of his mouth. If he expected a rebuke from Mary Forgan he was disappointed, but the older woman rose and crossed the floor to him, her troubled face alight with new interest.

'You arrived there in time to speak to my brother-in-law while he was still alive, Dan?'

'Oh, yes, Miss Mary. He had his faculties to the last. Although he had already been shot through the chest and knew he was dying, he knew what he wanted to say. He asked me to keep up with the work of enforcing the law. I was also to try and find out who our mutual enemy might be in this town, and also do all I could to protect his daughter.

'If it is of any interest to you, I can add that I intend to carry this fight with renegades further. He agreed with me that the Vernes attacked him. I shall not be satisfied until the gang are dead or in prison for a long time.'

Some aspect of the recent shock had rendered Della silent. It was not at all clear whether, in fact, she had heard what Dan said about his last exchanges with her father. On the other hand, Mary Forgan was on the alert. She escorted Dan to the front door, asking him one of two probing questions about the journey over the ridge and the gun exchanges. These he answered, clearly and with brevity. At the gate, he replaced his stetson and looked back.

Mary spoke first. 'You have a lot on your mind an' you're goin' to be very busy, but don't go around the town with the judge's death on your conscience. I'm sure that you did all that any ordinary man could in the circumstances, and more. Goodbye, Dan.'

The parting words warmed him. He wondered what sort of a reception he would get at the lawyer's office.

★ ★ ★

Hector March's law office was down the east end of the main street. Dan spent five minutes walking through to it and trying to avoid those who were avid for news. No sooner had he passed through the outer door than he was admitted to the inner, private office by a tall, thin, close-cropped clerk with hollow cheeks and a mild consumptive cough.

'The town marshal is here now, Mr March,' he murmured to the head of the firm, who was seated behind a formidable black-topped desk.

James H. Blane, minus his curly-brimmed hat and fiercely twirling his moustache, was seated in an arm-chair usually reserved for influential clients to the right of the local man. Dan seated himself opposite, availed himself of a small cigar offered and as he went through the motions of lighting it, he compared the two legal men briefed to appear at the trial of the town's three prisoners.

Hector March, who was to have

prosecuted in Judge Lacey's court, was some five years the older. His metal-rimmed spectacles and squarish dark beard with the grey highlights in it, made him look equally formidable, but perhaps a little less flamboyant.

'Blane, here, tells me we have a case to contest, but no judge to preside over it, Dan. I sure would be glad if you could give me, each of us that is, much of the detail of the judge's passin'. I hardly need to tell you that his death will have a profound effect upon more law offices than this one, apart from the community at large.'

'I'm sure you'd like to add the survivin' kin to your openin' remarks, Mr March, but I'll give you the facts you ask for. Incidentally, I'm involved as much as anyone.'

Dan's rather blunt reply had the effect of annoying both lawyers, but as he had a clear head and a straight-forward way of putting facts they soon forgot their displeasure and listened avidly to what he had to say about the ambush and after. He talked for upwards of five minutes. By the end of that time, both lawyers were sitting back and inwardly digesting what he had said. Blane, the visitor, continued to brood, his grey, bulbous eyes roving the room restlessly without seeing anything in particular.

'May I ask what you've done since you returned to town, Dan?' March asked, breaking the silence.

'I've checked in the office, spoken to my deputy and the jailer, and apart from talking with the women, Mr Blane here has contacted the doctor and the undertaker.'

Dan frowned suddenly, knowing that he had neglected to get in touch with the county sheriff by telegraph. He rose to his feet, wanting to put the matter right without delay.

'You haven't contacted the sheriff?' March guessed.

Dan admitted as much, and the lawyer commiserated with him, saying that a minute or so more would not make a whole lot of difference.

'What I want to know,' March went on, 'is how the case against the Ferrises and McGall is to progress. Do you still think justice will best be served by keeping them here until another qualified judge can be located and sent out to Redrock?'

At this point, Lawyer Blane seemed to come out of his prolonged reverie, but he was content to listen.

Dan said: 'I'm no longer convinced we ought to keep the prisoners here. Clearly, the Verne boys will strike again. I don't know that I want this town to suffer, if they come here. So I'd be in favour of sending the prisoners to the county seat.'

Wagging a big, spatulate finger, Blane objected. 'If it wasn't safe for my clients to be moved before, how can it be safe now?'

Dan showed a sudden flash of anger. 'In keepin' those three killers in town here, we were makin' sure they didn't escape justice. Believe me, Mr Blane, if they're moved in the near future, they'll be in no danger. It's the men detailed to escort them that might suffer, not them! In any case, I'm surprised to hear you talk that way after Judge Lacey's murder! I should have thought he was a friend of yours, seein' as how you come from Middleton.'

'A respected colleague,' Blane conceded, 'but not necessarily a friend.'

A minute later, Dan Marden left the office rather abruptly, and to his surprise he found his kid brother, Vance, listening wide-eyed to certain revelations being put to him by the regular clerk, who might conceivably have been eavesdropping.

Vance, at twenty-three, looked healthy, although his fresh-complexioned freckled face was covered in dust. He had his flat cream-coloured stetson in one hand while he mussed up his sandy hair with the other. Normally, his full face bore a rather ingenuous expression, but on this occasion when Dan's sudden appearance was taking him by surprise, the expression was altogether different. He had a cold, calculating look about him, as though he was far more concerned about how the judge's death would affect him rather than sorrowing for the old lawyer or worrying about Della.

Dan rightly judged that Vance had been on a long ride to some other law office in another town. But he was not keen to answer his brother's questions at that time. Remarking that he would see him later, at home, he walked through the outer office and came out on the street.

4

During the remaining hours of daylight, a posse came out from the county seat and explored the possible trails which the killers of Judge Lacey might have taken. Redrock was alive with sensational rumour and speculation about the trio of undesirables occupying the cells at the rear of the peace office.

Both lawyers sent long messages to the county seat in an effort to clear up the situation about the trial of the Ferrises and McGall. The wires were buzzing until a comparatively late hour. Supposedly in the dark about what had happened were the three prisoners, but even they had been informed of the recent events when a sly townsman had sidled up to their window on the outside and offered to trade them information for a silver dollar.

As the light started to fade the three

confederates argued their position loud and long. Food had long since been put through to them by the jailer and no one had been near them since the dirty pots had been taken away.

Rod Ferris, the undisputed leader of this trio, was a tall man in his late thirties, with a drooping brown moustache and a big nose which had been spread by another man's fist at a comparatively early age. He was the first to grow tired of speculation, and he retired into a corner of the cell which they all three used to contemplate the shadows and pick his gapped teeth with a matchstick.

Slim, the younger Ferris, who was also on the tall side and possessed a fleshy nose, argued on. His scarred hands frequently moved between belt level and his face, where he massaged the black tuft of chin beard which lengthened his countenance.

Jonas McGall, the third man in the cell, was in his early forties, although he did not look so old. He was a shorter, rotund, barrel-chested individual with small, restless, button-like eyes. His pleated plaid coat and the fur cap which adorned his round, greying head gave him the appearance of a trapper.

The prisoners slept fitfully throughout the night. Almost all the time one or another of them was awake, just in case an attempt was made to spring them out of jail. Nothing like that happened, however, and they were in a tricky mood when Bronc Malloy cautiously brought in their breakfast and slid it on a tray under the door.

Rod Ferris gave out with his low, wicked laugh. 'Oh, so it's you, Malloy. Ain't you scared to come near us now the judge has been eliminated?'

Malloy was more than a little scared about recent events, but he kept his true emotions well under control. 'Why should I be scared of you, Ferris? You didn't shoot the judge, even if you know who did it. You're jest as much a prisoner today as you were yesterday.

'Maybe I did you three jaspers a

51

favour, pickin' you up like I did when you was liquored. After all, in *this* county you're only wanted for robbery. If you'd stayed at large, you most likely would have been facing a more serious charge.'

'But if you'd left us alone, Malloy,' Slim argued, 'we wouldn't have been eatin' this poisonous prison food, would we?'

Malloy knew that he could not win this argument. He therefore prepared to withdraw. Slim shouted after him, but when McGall started to get more than his fair share of the food, young Ferris used his tongue in another direction.

Half an hour later, Dan Marden finished going through his mail and immediate paper work and walked through the cell corridor to talk with the trio. They surveyed him speculatively, as he seldom came their way and they knew little about him.

'Mornin', boys. Did you sleep well?'

Dan paused a foot or so away from the bars and looked them over. He thought they looked an unprepossessing bunch of fellows and hoped that their likes would never grace these cells again. And then he remembered that his days as town marshal might be numbered and he thought of other things.

'Did you come to take us out of cells, Marshal?' McGall asked.

Dan grinned. 'No, nothing so upsettin' as that. I wanted to tell you that seein' your fellow outlaws have interfered with the judge, we shall be bound to keep you in Redrock a little longer without trial. I regret the inconvenience, but you really can't blame the authorities for the wild ways of the Vernes.'

Dan edged back and looked as though he might be leaving again.

'Ain't it possible another judge will come out this way to try us?' the older Ferris asked, moving to the bars.

'I'd say it was unlikely,' Dan replied civilly.

'Then if no judge comes to us, they'll

have to move us,' McGall spat out at him.

Dan nodded and got as far as the door at the end of the corridor. Something seemed to happen to Slim Ferris at that moment.

'If you're jest tryin' to get on our nerves, Marshal, you're wastin' your time. We won't be here all that long. We aren't the first boys to be busted out of a peace office cell, an' don't you forget it!'

Dan turned on his heel and came back a yard or so. 'Are you thinkin' that window might be pulled out, Slim? I thought you were. Now you hear this. Judge Lacey was a close personal friend of mine. How would it be if I sent a masked man in the night to that window? You wouldn't know who it was until it was too late. He could shoot all three of you stone dead an' then make his escape before anyone was the wiser.

'That way you'd be dead, you'd have paid for your crimes. I could relax, the judge's death would be avenged, an' this town wouldn't have to keep payin' out money in expenses for scum the likes of you. How about that, Slim? Think it over, why don't you?'

In a deathly silence, Dan went through the door and locked it behind him. Several minutes elapsed before the affronted prisoners recovered from the shock which his bluff had given them, and even when they started to shout, they were not so confident as they had been.

★   ★   ★

It was towards two in the afternoon that Redrock began to assume the special aura of a Western town in mourning. The hollow-sounding tolling of the bell started it, and shortly afterwards those who were about to visit Boot Hill, the burial ground, on foot, began the slight ascent to the cemetery which was located on a high knoll.

Within minutes the main street filled with horses, carts and small, lightweight conveyances such as buggies and buckboards.

The troubled young marshal watched them go by, sharing the window of his office with his deputy and the old jailer, who was wearing a battered black hat and an arm band for the occasion.

'You'll be goin' to the burial yourself, won't you, Dan?' Shamus asked. His breath was tainted with whisky.

'Yes, I shall put in an appearance, Shamus, but it'll only be part of my duty on account of our cell residents and other considerations.'

Dan knew that Malloy was drinking in every word and wondering if the situation between the marshal and the Lacey girl had deteriorated any more. He glanced in the deputy's direction, and wondered if he had any plans to go up to Boot Hill.

'Bronc, I want you to give it about five minutes, and then begin a slow patrol on foot around the lesser streets. The last time we had a big funeral like this two or three shops were broken into and we never did find out who did it. You understand? Give this street a miss, and stick to the others. It ain't my intention that your prisoners should go amissin', if that's what you're wonderin' about.'

The deputy's saturnine face worked as he weighed up his instructions. Twice he looked as if he was going to raise a query or protest, but he thought better of it.

'All right, Dan. If you want me in a hurry, the usual gunshot signal will do the trick.'

Dan acknowledged the utterance and turned his attention to the jailer. 'In a little while, you may be the only law-abidin' hombre on this street, so make sure you don't go to sleep on the job, huh?'

Shamus protested, claiming that he had never done such a thing in his long years of service, but a sharp look from Dan quickly cut him short. With a long expiration of breath which might have been interpreted as a sigh, the marshal stepped out into the street. A few yards away, in an alley, he collected his dun riding horse.

★ ★ ★

Boot Hill was a big grassed triangle, a green patch over a useful mound commanding a view in the general direction of the centre of town. The horses and vehicles had already blocked one side of the approach track both before and beyond the cemetery by the time Dan rode his big-boned mount up the hill. At once, he was aware of the coolness among the walking mourners. Clearly, there were many people in Redrock who felt that he had done less than might have been expected of him in the unfortunate matter of the judge's demise.

For a time, as he waited beside his horse, Dan felt oppressed by their stares. It was only when the principal mourners and the hearse began to come up the slope that he felt himself again. Mary Forgan gave him a brief tight smile as a couple of elderly men stepped forward to help her to the ground. Della had on a wide-brimmed black hat which effectively hid her expression, but he had the feeling that it was hostile.

The daughter, her aunt and the servants slowly gravitated towards the place of burial. The undertaker and his short team of solemn-faced bearers followed them up close. There was a general removing of hats among the males in attendance and then a closing of the ranks about the grave as the parson assumed control with his mane of white hair shifting in a light breeze.

As the gentle movement began, Dan observed that his brother, Vance, left the side of his employer, Hector March, and stepped forward to take the elbow of Della, his intended. Again, the girl's face was in shadow, but something about the way she received Vance's attentions convinced all who were looking that they were welcome.

Some yards to the rear, where he had deliberately isolated himself, Dan felt a pang of envy. Years ago when they were very small he had fancied Della himself, and he still retained some affection for her, although of late he had played it down on account of Vance.

As the singing of the first hymn swelled out of the populace, Dan found himself wondering if Vance really deserved Della for his future wife. After all, in the matter of maturity there was far more than two years separating the two of them, and Vance would have to alter his ways very considerably if he was to make a responsible husband in the near future.

Again the young marshal felt pangs of jealousy. He turned his thoughts away from the burial and deliberately went over in his mind what he had planned for himself that afternoon. There would be many attending the funeral who would look upon his leaving the service as an act in bad taste, but he was determined to do it.

Five minutes later, he slipped away. He turned a slight bend in the downward track before mounting up and putting on his hat. His brief glimpse of the town centre had shown no signs of life whatever, and yet he knew that there would be some folk down there and not all of them would be sleeping in the heat of the day.

His plan was to keep a watch on the cells, so as to prevent any sort of rescue attempt from being successful. Having thought deeply that forenoon about how the outlaws could be freed, he had come to the conclusion that during the burial was the best opportunity. He was still of the same opinion. Nearing the first street, he kept the dun stepping as gently as possible.

He was making his approach to the rear of the peace office, working on the assumption that any strike would be made against the back, seeing as how the front office was occupied by the jailer. It seemed strange, hearing the muted voices up on the hill. The ambush attack by comparison seemed to be entirely foreign, a happening in another age.

At the end of Second Street, horses resting in the stalls of a livery shifted uneasily as he went by. A stray dog came to sniff at them, but a clap of the hands was sufficient to send it elsewhere. Twenty yards along, Dan slipped to the ground and walked the dun by the head, listening intently.

There were no sound clues to anything unusual. Directly across the backs from Main and his office, he slipped the riding horse into an alleyway beside a two-storey board building. At the outset it had been built as an hotel, but when it lacked the necessary support the owner quickly sold out to a speculator, and since then it had been used as offices.

Only the ground floor was used for business, and on this day everything was vacated. Dan, who had access to the building, headed into it and up a creaking wooden staircase with his

Winchester cradled under his right arm.

The windows of an upper rear office were so streaked and dirty that they might never have been cleaned since they were fitted. Dan was able to stand behind one and know that he would not be seen. He eased back his tight-fitting Stetson and mopped his brow and sideburns with his pale blue bandanna, which had been a gift from Della Lacey the year before. Next, he flexed his shoulders under the black vest which he wore habitually.

Sinking on to one knee, he lifted the lower half of a window and peered through it. The room in which he was standing for some reason had been built out over the ground floor. He found himself looking directly downward into the long narrow strip of comparatively useless ground between the office building and the rear of the peace office.

A brief scrutiny of the building he worked in gave him some satisfaction.

One of the prisoners tossed the butt end of a cigarette out through their barred window, a clear indication that they were still in residence. The stove-pipe gave no indication that a fire was burning in the boiler.

He wondered how Shamus was getting on, holding the office on his own with his known outsize thirst tearing at his guts. Dan had never thought that the old man would get through the afternoon without a spot of Forty-Rod, the local make of whisky. He did think, however, that Shamus would take it in with him and do his drinking on the premises.

Dan shifted his knee as the bones creaked in it. He began to wonder if his vigil ought to have been kept in a building alongside of the peace office, rather than in the next street. He was blinking his eyes and wondering afresh how the funeral was going when a very slight movement on Main caught his eye and tensed him up. A figure had crossed the narrow opening between the peace office and the weathered building next to it. A man had moved as though he was stepping up to the wooden sidewalk in front of the office.

Dan wished he could hear the exchanges between the newcomer and Shamus because he felt sure that the stroller had gone in and stayed there. The distance was far too great, of course. There were no other immediate developments, but this time the lack of incident made the happening seem more sinister.

Shamus Rent, moreover, was something of an unknown quantity on a hot afternoon.

5

A slight heightening in tension made Dan put his head out of the window and ease up the frame with the back of his shoulders. Shamus had his faults, but he would never willingly go along with anything like a jailbreak. Dan was coming to two conclusions, all built on the lack of noise. Either Shamus had been taken by surprise, or he wasn't in the building at all.

There was a sudden clamour of voices in the cell. Clearly, there was about to be a development of sorts. Distantly, a door clanged. Someone was about to visit the prisoners. Dan set his mobile mouth in a firm line and thought again of the three-man assault upon his deceased friend, the judge.

He sensed, rather than heard, the key going into the lock of the big door which gave access from the rear to the cell corridor. He knew that three locks must have been turned and he no longer doubted that the flitting figure he had seen meant trouble.

The outer door slowly swung outwards. The crowsfeet wrinkles in Dan's face tightened as he watched and speculated who would first be seen in the open. His trigger finger developed a small nervous tremor as a shadowy outline appeared. The emerging man cautiously detached himself from the corridor wall and stuck out his head.

There was no mistaking who it was. Rod Ferris. Tall, and looking taller in the grey bulky stetson which had suffered in the office. Ferris rubbed his flat nose and sniffed the outer atmosphere suspiciously. He blew out his brown moustache and suddenly gave a gusty, wolfish grin. His low, deadly laugh spanned the distance between the two buildings.

'It's all right, brother. Ain't nobody here waitin' to cut us down. Go fetch the rifles an' then we'll get a-goin'. This here is the route we'll take. So hurry it up, why don't you?'

Dan licked his dry lips. The cell break was on. No signs or sounds of the old man left in charge, nor of the individual who had manipulated the keys. Imminent gunplay, however, unless the would-be escapers gave in without a fight. The peace officer used a little will power to control his trigger finger.

Rod Ferris slipped back briefly into the passage and then came out again. He was desperately anxious to make tracks before any other developments could take place. He already had the twin guns with which he did most of his fighting. This time, he examined the fences and the buildings on either side, no doubt wondering where the nearest horses were located.

Dan let him advance for five to ten yards, and then he decided that the challenge ought to be made. He cleared his throat.

'Ferris! This is Town Marshal Marden callin' you! I have a gun lined up on you! Your escape bid is off, unless you want to die!'

It took just a couple of seconds for Ferris to find out where the challenging voice was located. As soon as he had seen Dan's head, his brain started to work. Obviously, he had decided upon defiance.

'Take it easy, Marden! You wouldn't dare shoot down men awaitin' trial, now would you?'

All the time he was shouting, Ferris was glaring this way and that, but in the main he was expecting a sharp reaction from his brother, who must surely have heard.

'Stay right where you are and drop those guns!'

This time, Dan's challenge had a note of unyielding authority in it. Rod Ferris, who had edged towards the farther fence, hesitated. He turned down the muzzles of his sixguns, which he had drawn. He appeared to be about to discard them. At the same time, the long figure of Slim was outlined in the doorway. Slim blasted off three quick rounds with a Spencer rifle, and then hurled himself out of the door and tossed a similar weapon across to his brother.

Dan had ducked, because the glass in the window above him had shattered. He blinked, doffed his hat and looked up again, keen to see the latest development. Both Ferrises were on the move. Rod was running down the side of his fence, blazing away with both six-guns at the window.

Fortunately, due to the running motion, the bullets were not as accurate as he was capable of. Besides, he had the rifle gripped under his armpit. Down the other side of the waste ground, Slim came forward at a loping run.

Dan had to make up his mind and seeing that his weapon was more or less trained upon the older brother, he adjusted his aim and carefully squeezed off the first shot. Rod's lurching run had the effect of making him miss. He fired another two before the outlaw reached the comparative safety of a line of trash cans, and still the escaper remained unscathed.

Dan frowned with concern. He was not doing very well, and any moment there might be three targets down there, instead of two. Slim hurled himself full length behind five or six large wooden packing cases which also afforded some shelter. The marshal, the only one who had started calm, was breathing heavily as though he had done all the running. His attention was claimed by the rear exit where the brothers had appeared. For several seconds he anticipated the appearance of Jonas McGall, but the barrel-chested outlaw was slow to appear.

And there were no signs of the man who had opened the cell door. Dan was thinking rather irrelevantly that this sudden outburst of gunfire on the occasion of the burial must be having a signal effect upon the mourners.

While he still squinted purposefully

at the point of exit, the brothers opened up on him simultaneously. All he could do was duck his head and hope that something would happen quickly to change the present state of affairs. Shards of glass flew and the bullets whined and homed into the woodwork. He had started the shooting, but the outlaws had taken over with a vengeance.

Presently his brain started to function clearly again. Neither of the brothers showed any inclination to go back to the cell corridor and make a fresh exit through the front of the peace office: so, they had to keep coming towards Second Street.

Dan gripped his Winchester and rolled sideways, heading for the other window located in the same office. It had occurred to him that if he was not careful one or other of his adversaries might make off on his own dun, and that would be a loss of face he just could not stand.

He had to use what brief period of

surprise he could muster and try to eliminate one of them. Breathing hard, he punched out glass with his gun muzzle. This happened just as Slim leapt over the top of his packing cases and dived for the shelter of the lower part of the building. For a split second, Dan had him in his sights, and that was sufficient for a telling shot. The Winchester kicked against his shoulder and he continued to look down at the moving man. Slim appeared to halt in his stride and then, weaving in rather an incredible fashion, he started to go down with the bullet through his forehead.

Dan's respite was short-lived. Rod fired two shots at him and the second one struck the barrel of the Winchester near the muzzle, mildly jarring his hands. He dropped it and pulled his revolver, shifting his position and aiming it without delay.

In his turn, Rod Ferris ducked out of sight. The Colt continued to bark and the shells from it ripped into the metal of the trash cans, making them leap an inch or two at a time. When Dan's revolver was empty, he took a deep breath and pulled back a bit from his exposed position.

If Rod planned to make a break for the building, now was his chance. No one emerged from the corridor. All quiet in that direction. Hastily Dan began to reload. He willed himself to be calm as he pulled revolver bullets out of his belt and thumbed them into the cylinder. He finished his reloading and still Ferris did not move.

Soon, there would be others heading for the area of the exchanges and the chances of the outlaws would diminish. Dan hastily brushed perspiration from his sideburns and his forehead. He wondered what the outcome would be. And where were the two other men? McGall and the mysterious stranger were taking things all too quietly, if they had not already cleared out.

Rod Ferris must have been thinking similar thoughts. All at once, the balance changed. An arm appeared at the rear exit, pushing further open the door, which had swung part way shut. In the mere second or so that it took for Dan to adjust to the new factor, Rod Ferris was up on his feet and running forward.

Yelling to himself, Dan stood up and raked the glass out of the second window. The brief delay was all that was necessary for the outlaw to make the final piece of cover along the length of the open ground. Ferris dived behind a low pile of thick wooden planks, not unlike railway ties or sleepers.

Dan fired a snap shot at the exit door, heard it clang off the metal grille and was reassured for the moment when the third figure withdrew. At once, the marshal shifted his target, blasting at the near end of the wooden ties. In his present position he could not get a good shot at his victim, even though the piles were not stacked very high.

This called for taking a chance. He

heaved up the window and put the upper part of his trunk outside, bringing up the Winchester in readiness. This time, he had to be accurate — and lucky.

Once again the exit door swung. Dan looked for a figure and saw none. He steeled himself to keep his attention on the wooden ties and had to duck uncomfortably when Ferris's gun muzzle briefly lanced flame in his direction.

In ducking, Dan saved himself from being wounded, but he also experienced the troubled sensation which accompanied loss of balance. He had too much of his body and his weight outside the window. He dug in desperately with his boot toes, but that did not have the desired stabilising effect. For a few seconds, he fought desperately before tilting forward and downwards in a slow somersault which had him fearful of the outcome. While he was on the way down to the dust and hard ground below, Ferris, who had also been very surprised by this development, fired and missed.

The outlaw slowly rose from behind the low ties which had severely cramped his activities, but he was slow to take the advantage of lining up his weapon on the falling body. A series of distant shouts blended in with the general turbulence and gave Ferris something else to think about.

Miraculously, Dan landed squarely upon the flat of his shoulder blades. Even so, he was shaken and bruised and for a few seconds he did not realise that he still had his Winchester clutched in his hand. He rolled painfully on to his chest, breathing as if his lungs were overworked, and slowly lined up the weapon on the crouching, hesitant figure before him.

Ferris called: 'Hey, McGall, what in tarnation is keepin' you? Let's go, before it's too late! We won't get another opportunity after this!'

Dan's blurred vision cleared. He aimed at Rod Ferris and squeezed.

Dust clouded his vision, but he managed to clear his eyes in time to see the stricken man sink backwards against the fence, holding his chest and losing his weapon. Ferris's expression looked hopeless.

McGall's rather distinctive voice yelled the dying outlaw's name. This was sufficient warning to make Dan roll again and line up his shoulder weapon on the door. To his surprise, the man in the plaid coat did not seem to know what to do for the best. McGall hesitated, stepping back rather than forward, although his rifle was to hand and all he had to do was raise it and fire.

Against the slight shadow around the door, Dan did not expect to be very accurate. He lined up on the dark rectangular opening and prepared to take on the third man. The three shots that followed, however, came from the corridor. At first it seemed that McGall must have fired them, but this was not the case.

Dan rose to his knees and remained that way for a few seconds when the third man staggered back to the door, half raised a hand — almost as though in a kind of salute — and then toppled forward into the dust of the open air. He was already dying.

Distantly, the sounds of men on the move were clearly heard. Those who planned to take a hand in whatever was going on were sorting themselves out from the women and wondering how long it would take for them to get back into town and to their weapons. Few failed to guess at the cause of the gun exchanges.

Dan rose to his feet; weaving slightly, he moved forward with his Winchester trained on the door. He felt that he had taken all the surprises he could cope with in such a short time. And yet the next one might be critical, and therefore it was essential to stay on the alert.

One thing was certain, McGall had not been shamming when he fell forward into the open air. Someone else with a gun was on the alert and active, indoors. Dan persisted in this belief, until the dark corridor swallowed him. The keys were still in the cell door. Of the mystery man who had engineered the escape there was no sign. The place was deserted. Even the cat which Shamus fed had vacated its afternoon dozing spot near one wall, no doubt leaping through the street side window which had been left open at the top.

Dan returned to the rear. He was still a little stunned, although all the action had gone his way. He studied the leaking holes in McGall's back and decided that he had been shot three times at close range with a hand gun. Something made him think it was a .44, but he had no special reason for making such a guess.

He hauled McGall back into the corridor, checked that his pulse had failed altogether, and was just going in search of the other two corpses when

Shamus Rent reappeared looking very sheepish.

'Dan, I sure am sorry I took off like I did, but . . . well, are you all right?'

'Sure I'm all right, Shamus, but no thanks to you! I've been on the receivin' end of three guns or more.' Dan blinked. For the life of him he was not sure if he had named the right number of weapons, but he felt it did not matter unduly at that moment. 'Come on out the back an' help me get the other stiffs indoors. I have a feelin' it'll be better that way. Can't say why at the moment, though.'

Having been reassured that all three outlaws were dead, Shamus willingly loaned his strength to the moving of the bodies. While they toiled to get them indoors, Dan asked a question or two.

'Did you see anybody leavin' the office as you came along? I mean when the shootin' finished.'

'Nope. Nobody at all, Dan. Shucks, are you sayin' that some hombre sneaked in here while I was away slakin' my thirst and deliberately took the keys and unfastened those three jaspers?'

'That's about the size of things, old timer,' Dan panted as they struggled indoors with the third body, that of Rod Ferris. 'Now, there'll be men in here, pronto, askin' a lot of foolhardy questions. There's one I have to ask you before they come. Did you shoot Jonas McGall to make up for leavin' the office?'

The old jailer looked crestfallen and deeply hurt. 'Ain't never shot a man in the back in my life, Dan, an' that's for sure. Maybe you'd like to examine my gun? It ain't been fired!'

Dan blinked as Shamus slowly hauled his long-barrelled weapon out of its holster. He shook his head and noticed that earlier shooting pains brought on by his fall had left him.

'That won't be necessary, Shamus. Take the keys and make the rounds. Lock that corridor exit door first. Pretty soon, we'll have to answer a lot of questions. I ain't sure that I can do a lot of talkin' unless I have something to cut the dust in my throat.'

Shamus's spirits began to revive. 'I understand, Dan. I'll lock up an' then I'll mosey off an' find you something. A spot of Forty-Rod, maybe. Then, if there's time, I'll see if I can find your hat. Is there any special way you want me to talk to the lawyers an' all?'

Dan thought about Blane and March. They would surely be along in the van of the male mourners, as their work would now be affected again.

'Let me do the talkin' for a start,' he suggested. 'By the way, my hat is in the office building over on Second. You'll see the missin' glass out of the windows.'

As men's feet came down the sidewalk, Dan picked up a dark piece of curtain and began to pin it up over the street window.

6

Suddenly the door opened, and Deputy Bronc Malloy, the first of several men who had a right to be there at that time, advanced into the room. Dan had just lighted a lamp, having hung the window drape in place to prevent sightseers from looking in.

'Everything all right, Dan?' Bronc asked.

'Sure, there's been an attempted breakout, but everything's back to normal now. Stand by the door, will you? I don't want all the town in here.'

Dan sounded brusque, and Malloy wondered if his attitude was justified. A brief examination of the marshal's guns, temporarily discarded, seemed to suggest that he had been very busy. Even with Malloy on the door, several persons managed to get inside. First came James Blane and Hector March, the two lawyers, breathing heavily and looking around suspiciously.

Dan nodded to them and motioned for them to stand aside. Following them came the town's doctor, veteran medical man Mervyn Floyd, a native of Wales who had looked to be around sixty-three years of age for as long as Dan could remember. Floyd was tall; neatly dressed in a dark suit. His white beard, trimmed short, and thin-rimmed spectacles added to the impression given by his hard, deadpan expression. The eyes behind his lenses, however, were alert enough.

Dan wanted Bronc to close the door for good, but Egil Berg, the town's big florid Scandinavian mayor, was still to come, and lastly Shamus Rent re-entered with a flat liquor bottle half-hidden in the palm of his hand.

Out in the street, men called loudly to one another. The uproar increased in volume, and men in the office who wanted information looked as if they might add to it. It was a toss up who would demand to know all the details first. Dan, for once, surprised the influential people who had come to see him by crossing in front of them and receiving the whisky bottle from Shamus's somewhat shaky hand.

'Is it the best?' he asked tersely.

Shamus, who was overawed by the gathering and the coming investigation, nodded rather vigorously and assured Dan that none better could be obtained anywhere in the county. Dan nodded, uncorked it, and tipped a generous measure down his throat. He was slow to pause, and when it was clear that he was not going to invite anyone to join him, the temporary surprised calm in the room came to an end.

Egil Berg cleared his fleshy throat and patted his well-filled white vest with his big ostler's hand. He had a permanent scowl upon his face which deepened when he had to make a speech.

'Marshal, things have been happening here at a most unseemly time. Folks inside and outside of this office want an explanation. If you intend to run again for marshal, you'd be well advised not to keep us in the dark too long.'

Berg's bulk towered to a full three inches above Dan, who looked the mayor over rather thoughtfully, starting at the top of his flashy cream stetson, and working down past the eye-catching white vest and ending up with the riding breeches and leggings.

'Mr Berg, who am I to keep the good people of Redrock in the dark? You're a speech-maker. Could I ask you to step out into the open and inform the general public that there has been an attempted breakout which has failed? Tell the folks that the forces of law and order have prevailed and that the prisoners are back in custody.'

Berg sniffed. He glared at Dan and then at the doctor as if that worthy's poker face would reveal anything not yet mentioned. The lawyers were not happy with the way things were going, and something in their attitude communicated itself to the mayor, who did not really like being looked over the way Dan did it on account of his yearly increase in weight.

'Marden, I'm not satisfied. Before I do as you request, I'd like to see the prisoners. Be so good as to open the door of the cell block and let me see for myself.'

There was a general edging forward as Dan reached for the key ring and stepped to the door which opened on to the corridor. Shamus was the only one who did not press forward. With a flourish, Dan opened the door and stepped back. Beyond it, the three corpses were laid out on the floor, side by side.

The newcomers gasped as they saw them and, after the briefest of hesitations, they stepped through the door to take a closer look. Heading them was the poker-faced doctor who apparently could smell blood. Malloy was the last man to step through the opening, and his eyes met those of Dan in a backward glance as he followed the others.

'Step to the street door an' say the mayor will make a statement in a minute, Shamus.'

The old man did as he was told. Dan went through to join the others and at once they hemmed him in, calling loudly for answers. Only the doctor stayed low over the corpses, sorting out the way they had died with long spatulate fingers and white cuffs which never somehow were tainted with blood.

'I anticipated that the burial time was the best time for such an attempt as has been made. I covered this building from the office block on Second, and sure enough, first the older Ferris and then the younger came out at the back.

'The keys had been turned by a stranger I haven't identified yet who came in through the front of the office while the anchor man of my staff was out on a little errand.'

'I don't like this at all,' Lawyer Blane boomed ominously.

'Neither do I,' March agreed, with feeling.

Berg was trying to think up words in which to condemn the marshal's conduct when the voice from below remarked: 'This man here, McGall, I believe he was called. Shot in the back three times! Messy, to say the least.'

Berg opened his mouth again, but Dan forestalled him.

'Mayor, I'd like you to step out into the street and tell the local people that the prisoners are back indoors. You don't have to tell them at this time that they are all dead. If you could keep that information from them at this stage I'd be obliged. You see, there's a lot to sort out yet. Whether they'll be kept in this town now that the judge and they are dead, and other considerations.'

Already, the bulky mayor, who was perspiring steadily in the confined space, was starting to shake his head. 'I can't do that. Ain't no reason for keepin' such everyday information from ordinary townsfolk who have a right to know. Maybe I ought to get on out there and tell them everything. I wonder what you other gents feel about this?'

Berg began to push his way out, not waiting to hear the lawyers' views. Dan gave ground for him and unexpectedly grinned.

'Suit yourself, Mayor. Tell 'em all, if that's what you want. Only you'll find yourself hearin' a lot of questions you can't answer. I haven't had the time to do any investigatin' myself.'

'Why do you want the matter of their deaths kept from the locals?' Blane asked, grudgingly.

'Because I have a feelin' that these three dead outlaws might lead us to the rest of the gang they belong to, and those others, the killers of the judge, are much more formidable than this trio.'

A certain amount of blinking and nodding went on between the two lawyers. It was as though they were able to converse in mimed code. As Berg paused with his heavy hand on the handle of the street door, March called after him.

'We think Marshal Marden may have a point, Mayor. Maybe you ought to tell it *his* way.'

Dan felt a certain amount of anger welling up inside of him, although he was about to get his way. He called: 'Sure, go ahead, Mayor! What have you to lose? You can always give the folks a scapegoat at a later hour, if anything goes wrong!'

Berg glared at him and stepped out into the street. This was the moment when the lawyers expected to learn all the known facts, and Dan did not disappoint them in the way he shaped up to business. Rent was the first man to be questioned.

'Now, Shamus, will you be good enough to tell me and the assembled gentlemen how you allowed yourself to be enticed out of this office?'

Dan sat on the end of his desk and

busied himself with a tobacco sack. He did nothing to make the old man's task any easier. Rent coughed to clear his dry throat.

'All my life I've been afflicted with thirst, an' when this quiet hombre tossed an eagle through the open window and suggested I ought to get along to the nearest saloon an' slake my thirst I thought the heavens had opened.

'You'll allow everything was quiet. You could almost hear the words of the service up on the hill. At first, my conscience was against me leavin' the office an' I murmured something to that effect through the window.'

'Who was the man who threw in the money?' Malloy demanded bluntly.

Shamus shrugged. 'A stranger, I guess. He kept in the shadows outside. I never did get to see his face or anything.'

'Did he argue with you?' Dan queried calmly.

'He said if I didn't get out of that

office in ten seconds flat he was a-comin' in to recover what was rightfully his! Well now, that made me think. An elderly jailer like me has to work for a long time to earn the value of a golden eagle, so I called back to him that I would do it.

'He didn't answer, so when I stepped out into the street I looked around for him. He had stepped out of sight, probably into the alleyway.'

Clearly, the lawyers and the deputy thought that the old man had committed an error of judgement. Blane was about to say so, but the jailer spoke first.

'I didn't think there was any sort of threat to the security because there were no signs of any ridin' horses in the street or anywhere near. So, as I said, I took the money and the slight risk, an' I was found wantin'. I'd like to know who tossed in the coin as much as the rest of you. He very likely has cost me my job.'

Dan yawned, while the other listeners

mulled over what had been said. Out in the street, the mayor's dull, monotonous voice was giving out the bare facts. He was getting a few catcalls because he was not universally popular, but no one thought he might be lying or keeping back anything vital.

'How about you, Bronc? You were instructed to make a circuit of the town, keeping to the outskirts. At the time, I remember you thought my instructions were faulty. You mentioned coming at the run in the event of a gun signal. I was too busy to fire off a proper signal, but everyone in the neighbourhood must have heard the gun exchanges.

'You know what I'm getting at, I'm sure. You didn't arrive until all the shootin' was over. What kept you?'

Malloy had looked confident enough when the questioning started, but now he was not so sure. He felt he saw a small measure of suspicion in the eyes of Hector March.

'I did exactly what you told me, Dan.

I stayed around the perimeter. When the first shootin' happened I was crossin' the south end of town. I could tell straight away somethin' was happenin' near to here. So I got to thinkin' how best I could stop an attempt to free the prisoners. Like Shamus, I thought about horses. As we all know, the mayor has three liveries in the town. I recollected that the horses belonging to the prisoners had been left in the stable at the east end of Main. So I took myself along there and prepared to ambush anyone who came lookin' for those mounts. Only nobody came. And that's all I have to say.'

Clearly, the doctor and the two lawyers felt that he had vindicated himself by his actions. Bronc backed off and built himself a home-rolled cigarette. There was a light in his eye which suggested that his confidence was at a high level.

Out of doors, the indications were that the mayor's discourse was coming to an end. Dan shrugged and drew aside the two lawyers. The doctor followed them to stay within earshot, unbidden.

'Gents, Jonathan Lacey expected me to fight the Vernes out in the open, I feel sure. The judge's death was only a delayin' tactic. Now we've had this attempt to break the prisoners out of jail. Today's happenings prove that the Vernes are still interested in those three would-be escapers back there, even if we don't know all the facts.

'Contrary to what the mayor thinks, I'm not all that keen on servin' another term of office. I feel drawn to clearin' up the unfinished business which started on the other side of Coyote Ridge.'

'Am I right in thinkin' you want to use those three corpses to get near to the Vernes?' Blane asked bluntly.

'The corpses may be our only lead to the other outlaws,' Dan pointed out. 'Of course I'm interested in usin' them. You would, too, in my place. What I want to do is have the authorities in the county seat send for the trio as though they were still alive. I believe that by shipping them out we could draw the Vernes into the open.'

March, who had been looking forward to prosecuting the three dead men, cleared his throat. 'You may very well be right in your supposition, but if these villainous outlaws show up on trail, won't it put the lives of the sheriff's men at some peril?'

'It would, if the sheriff's men handled the assignment. But I wouldn't do it that way. I'd have the escort made up of men from Redrock. Men who knew and admired the judge, and who would be willin' to take a few risks on his behalf.'

After a brief silence, during which Mayor Berg came back into the room and mopped himself down, Blane and March appeared to accept in principle Dan's plan of action. Dr Floyd was blinking slowly behind his spectacles, a sure sign that he approved of the strategy. As the mayor kept silent, Malloy spoke up.

'It would need the tumbleweed wagon. You couldn't attempt to take dead men along on horseback. The driver of the wagon would be in danger all the way back to the county seat.'

'He would if he had to drive, Bronc,' Dan returned calmly. 'Most likely, though, I'd take over from him when he got to this town. Right now, I'd say the legal brains assembled here have approved my scheme, so I'd like *you* to go along to the telegraph office and send a message to the county sheriff, informing him of our decision to move the prisoners.'

Malloy, who was not at his best when putting together important written messages, looked as though he was going to protest. He decided to stay quiet, however, when Hector March followed up Dan's suggestion.

'Here's a pencil and paper. On behalf of Blane and myself, I'd like you to send a message to the county attorney's office in Middleton. Think you could take it down?'

Bronc was a long time getting into the desk chair, and when he blinked at the spelling of certain words, Dan took over from him and roughed out the two messages himself. The deputy's sallow complexion was heightened with extra colour as he received the two written messages and prepared to take them along for transmission.

Shortly after that, Dr Floyd left. He had promised to ask the undertaker to step along to the peace office after dark without informing anyone else what his purpose was.

The lawyers took Egil Berg along with them, fussing him a little like the thorough-going professionals they were. Dan felt certain that when they had done with him he would not make any premature revelations that could spoil the hastily conceived plans for the future.

That night he slept in the office, not bothering to go home to the board shack which he shared with Vance on the low side of town.

7

Dan Marden was long in getting off to sleep that night, due to the alarming events of the day and his half-formed plans for the future. When he did get off, however, he slept soundly and awoke refreshed some time after six o'clock.

He turned over his responsibilities to Shamus Rent and left the office in search of food within a half-hour. He was the Swedish café proprietor's first customer and his ham and eggs were well cooked. Towards the end of his meal, the owner, whose name was Larsen, started to ask questions about the shootings round about the peace office and that was Dan's signal to get on the move.

Without actually divulging anything new, he answered a couple of questions before leaving the building and making his way by a devious route to the shack he shared with his brother. Vance, when he was at home, was a heavy sleeper who usually slept late.

There was no sound coming from the building as Dan approached and he found himself walking on tiptoe so as not to disturb Vance. There was no sign of the younger brother in the big living-room, nor in the kitchen and wash-room which made up one end. Assuming that Vance was in bed in the one downstairs bedroom, Dan slipped into the most comfortable chair — one which had come from their family home — and took time out to smoke a cigarette. A plume of smoke was curling fitfully upwards towards the loft when Vance started to come up from the narrow creek, whistling to himself.

This brought Dan back to the present. He leapt to his feet, looked in the bedroom as though he could not believe his ears, saw the ruffled bed and then repaired to the door to meet his brother. Vance came up the slight slope with his eyes on the ground. He looked well groomed. His cream stetson had been brushed and he had on a white shirt under his jacket which looked to be brand new.

'Good mornin', brother,' Dan remarked easily.

'Why, howdy, Dan, I didn't expect to see you around at this early hour of the mornin'. Was there somethin' special you wanted?'

'I've already eaten. I wanted to collect a few things because I might be away for a while. And I reckoned you an' I hadn't talked seriously together for a long time.'

Vance patted him on the back as they stepped indoors. 'I hear you were good an' busy yesterday, holdin' off the three outlaws. Why don't you tell me about it while you take a shave?'

Dan nodded. For the first time since he left the peace office he told how he had fought with the outlaws, and about the mystery man who had almost brought about their escape.

'You got any ideas who it might be, the man who unlocked the doors, Dan?'

'None whatsoever. I sure would like to meet him, though, because he might lead me to Long John Verne and others.'

Dan's expression changed as he saw Vance's thoughtful face in the mirror. The latter remarked: 'It sure would mean a lot to you, to bring in the Verne boys, wouldn't it, Dan?'

'You're too darned right it would! After all, they did kill your future father-in-law an' caused a whole heap of trouble in this area. But you don't need to bother your head about that. The judge dyin' won't interfere with your plans, will it?'

'I might have to leave for law school in Tennessee sooner than I expected,' Vance explained calmly.

'But goin' off to law school is something you've always planned to do, so that's no surprise! March and the judge, they talked you into it together a long time ago. Am I right in thinkin' you're not keen to go?'

Dan finished scraping his chin and turned to face his brother, looking him straight in the eye.

A broad smile flashed on and off Vance's face. Dan had seen it many times before. He had seen it flashed with a negative answer and also with a positive one.

'The fact is, Dan, I ain't keen to leave, so I might as well tell you. It'll be a long, hard slog over there in law school, an' that sort of thing takes up a whole lot of a man's youth.'

Dan raised his brows. Vance had seldom spoken to him recently in this serious fashion. He wondered if his brother was beginning to mature at last.

'Tell me, are you reluctant to leave on account of leavin' Della at the same time?'

Vance chuckled. 'Maybe so. Maybe I jest like Redrock an' don't hanker for a far-off state. Maybe I jest don't cotton on to a whole lot of bookwork, Dan. I really couldn't say. I don't know myself all that well. Look, if it's all right to you, I'll get on into town now.

'I promised to be in the office early because this afternoon is somehow special. The judge's will is to be read, an' I have to be there. So I'll see you later, huh?'

Dan nodded and grinned and walked to the outside door after him, all the time wiping his hands and face on a square of cotton towel. He was thinking that maybe after all Redrock had another capable lawyer in the making.

★ ★ ★

The official vehicle for moving prisoners, known throughout the county as the tumbleweed wagon, arrived in Redrock pulled by four mature and rather ill-assorted horses at a little after six o'clock that evening.

The only man with the wagon, a mahogany-skinned ex-buffalo skinner known to all by the one name,

Arkensaw, was only too glad to get down off the box and stretch his legs in the dust of the street. He had been travelling since dawn on account of his boss saying that the journey had to be pushed.

Dan collared him as soon as he came down and took him off to a remote corner of the nearest saloon, where he started to put him in the picture. Within five minutes, in fact as soon as Arkensaw knew that the prisoners were dead, and that he was not being pressed to drive the meat wagon all the way back to the county seat with them inside, the new arrival started to lose his tenseness and relax.

When they had drunk three whiskies each, Arkensaw became thoughtful.

'Dan, this business of roundin' up the judge's killers sure must mean a lot to you. Especially at a time like this, when you want to be in town and chattin' up the folks so they'll vote for you again for a new term.'

Dan patted the driver on the

shoulder. 'Oh, I don't know, Ark. A change is a good thing, an' I don't appear to have as many friends in this neck of the woods as I thought. I stood off the Ferrises all right, but nobody came along to congratulate me. So I figure I'm due for a change.'

Arkensaw, who was also of an independent frame of mind, commiserated with him. They might have disposed of more liquor, but Dan saw Vance hovering about in the entrance and he chose to leave the driver to his own devices while he heard about the special meeting.

As soon as the brothers were out in the open, they headed for their shack. Vance waited until they were clear of other strollers and then opened up.

'The judge was well off, Dan. He left nigh on thirty thousand dollars to Della, and another five to Mary Forgan. As far as I'm concerned, he left me five hundred dollars.'

Vance's voice tailed off a little as he came to the matter of his own benefit.

Dan, who was grinning broadly, was surprised.

'Did you expect more? It's for your studies, isn't it? Won't it cost you a whole lot more than five hundred to keep yourself for two or three years an' pay for your studies?'

'It surely will, Dan, but you see, Hector March has been paying me five to ten dollars a week over and above my ordinary wages with the law firm, so that I could save the rest. I'm supposed to have enough to cover all expenses by now.

'I can have the money in the morning, provided I pull out straight away and head for Tennessee. Seems a bit sudden, don't you think?'

'Oh, sure, it's sudden, but lawyers and legal documents make things seem that way. Believe me, it's for the best.'

They called at home and Dan produced a small bottle of whisky from a secret place. They took it down to the water's edge and slowly drank a few fingers while they talked of this and that, reminiscing about the past and guessing at the future. The more they talked, the more certain Dan became that he and Redrock, even the whole county perhaps, were in for a lot of trouble before the vicious influence of the Vernes was finally removed.

At the end of a brief interval, he found that he had advice to give.

'Vance, you'll think I'm tryin' to push you to leave before it's necessary. But I have to leave with that tumbleweed wagon at an early hour. I'd feel better about what I have to do if I knew you'd already left town and were on your way. Now, what do you say?'

'I don't quite follow what you're askin', Dan, other than for me to hit the trail at daybreak. Is that what you're askin' me to do?'

Dan sighed. 'I guess it is, brother. But you could do it. You could get March to make over the five hundred dollars to you tonight so that you wouldn't have to wait for the office to open, and then you could take your farewell of Della. I don't suppose she'll want to get up at the crack of dawn to see you on your way, will she?'

Vance tossed a couple of small stones into the water and watched the ripples grow wider until they touched both banks.

'I suppose I could ask for the money tonight, if you think that's the best course of action. All right. I'll go back an' see March in a half-hour. He's still in the office. But about that tumbleweed job, Dan. Do you have to be the one to go along with the wagon?'

Slowly, they came to their feet. 'I gave my word because we'll be buckin' trouble, Vance. Sure, I have to be there. But I've taken chances before an' it hasn't seemed to bother you. Why should it this time?'

As they walked back towards the shack, Dan pressed Vance for an answer, but to his surprise his younger freckled brother had become totally uncommunicative. When they parted in front of the shack, Vance seemed to be under some strange stress.

Dan could not weigh it up at all. Vance's sudden change of mood had thoroughly surprised him. Was he really worrying himself into a state of nerves over his — Dan's — potential difficulties with three dead outlaws, or was his attitude something to do with those other doubts, the ones about leaving Redrock and taking up prolonged studies?

After sitting upon the narrow gallery for some ten minutes or more, Dan gathered a few essential things together and slowly plodded back into town. He was resolved to take his early start from the peace office, in the morning.

8

The measuring up for coffins had proved that the undertaker and several of his assistants could keep a secret, inasmuch as the preparatory work on the corpses had had to be done in the rear of the peace office instead of in the undertaker's parlour or in a private dwelling.

In order to get out the coffins and put them aboard the tumbleweed wagon undisturbed and unobserved by members of the general public, the actual loading began before dawn. Moving about near the office at that searching hour were Mayor Berg, who wanted to impress others, the two lawyers, Deputy Malloy, Shamus Rent, Arkensaw and the undertaker and his men.

Malloy and Rent were keeping watch some yards down the street from the peace office in either direction, hoping to head off or distract any early wayfarer who came to see what was happening. Fortunately, however, no one did come along during the time when the coffins were removed from the office and deposited in the wagon.

Dan was enjoying a last cigarette, closely flanked by the two lawyers, when Vance came along the street mounted on his usual riding horse, a black gelding, and leading a neat bay mare to the back of which his luggage was strapped.

Shamus Rent showed surprise when Vance arrived, but he quickly gave ground when Dan exhibited pleasure over the encounter. Side by side, the brothers walked the boards in front of the peace office for a minute or two, knowing that they might not meet again for quite a long time.

'You've got your route planned, Vance?' Dan asked.

'Oh, yes, I have the details I need, Dan. March's regular office clerk reads maps as a hobby. He had it all worked for me last evenin'. I'm crossin' the county south of Middleton, and heading for either Saddler's Ford or Eastberg, as you might have expected. I should hit the border between Arkansas and Louisiana shortly after crossin' the Red River. But you don't want to know all the details.

'I don't rightly know what to say to you, now that the time has come. I'm leavin' early, like you suggested. You'll most likely be headin' into trouble an' I won't know the outcome, seein' as how I'll be well to the east already.'

Pangs of affection made Dan stop short in his pacings. He gripped his brother by the shoulders. 'It's good to know you care, Vance. I can't say how things will turn out, of course. Around this time of day a man tends to be lookin' on the gloomy side. Maybe things will improve for me. As for you, I hope the right sort of life opens up for you. Della is a fine girl, even if she's a bit uppitty. You know what I mean?'

'I know what you mean, an' I don't rightly know how everything will turn out. Maybe the next time our paths cross we'll be able to look on the bright side. Anyways, it's time for me to push off. *Adios*, Dan, an' here's hopin' you'll always have a speedy draw.'

In the shadows, they gripped hands and parted at the outset of what was to prove another trying day for them. Dan boosted Vance into the saddle and stood in the middle of the dirt street while his only kin went off down the thoroughfare towards the east. As soon as Vance had turned a corner, Dan became impatient. All delays were bad for his enterprise. Although he did not care for the mayor, he forced himself to shake hands with Berg, who had in hand the business of sending the special riders on their way at a later hour. Berg, too, was embarrassed, but he managed to mutter a few words of encouragement as Dan mounted to the box of the prison van.

'Ain't no knowin' how the day will

turn out, friends,' he called down to the others, 'but here's hopin' I see the welcome sign of Redrock again before long.'

Amid the muted farewell greetings of the other men, he kicked off the brakes and rather noisily cracked the whip over the backs of the veteran horse team. This particular vehicle seemed to be heavy on its wheels, but it went forward fairly smoothly as soon as the team had got rid of their early morning wind and settled down to pull together.

The bright forks of dawn were ripping the shroud of darkness in the eastern sky as the grey-painted wagon rolled east and then turned north up the substantial trail which led indirectly towards the county seat. If all went well, the journey would be a long steady pull from dawn to dusk. But Dan did not expect all to go well. If he made half the distance without encountering trouble, he would be very surprised. This was one journey he did not expect to complete and, for once, it mattered very little to him if he actually lost his charges.

As the sky slowly brightened on his right, Dan was assailed by several yawns, but gradually he began to feel a sense of well-being. No one expected any sort of ambush this near to town, and his rearguard would be within striking distance before very long.

He found the sort of progress which the wagon made boring. For the life of him he could never have taken on as a regular driver as Arkensaw had done. Rather belatedly, he wondered why he had not invited his brother to go along with him part of the way.

Vance could only be a few miles ahead of him, as travellers whose general direction was east always followed a few miles of the northbound trail before turning off at the eastbound fork. Dan thought about Vance some more. Obviously, he had applied himself reasonably well in routine duties in the legal office, but just how good was his brain? How would he make out when he had to spend most of the day absorbing information from old and dusty legal volumes presided over by ancient practitioners of the legal profession?

Dan knew that he personally could never be a lawyer. He did not have the sort of presence a man must have for arguing a case in court. Whether Vance had that sort of style only time would tell.

The dappled rump of one of the nearer team horses had the effect of making Dan drowsy. He blinked hard and shifted his attention, and almost at once he started to hear the approach of the first traveller in the opposite direction. All this day, he reasoned, he had to be on the alert. Therefore, he checked his weapons: the Winchester under the seat and the Colt in his holster.

Approaching him quite quickly from the north was a rider on horseback. That much his ears told him without difficulty. He was alert for any sort of trickery, but he would not have guessed who it was.

Della Lacey had on a dark grey riding skirt and an unbuttoned coat to match. She was riding a dappled mare on a lightweight saddle and apparently getting some pleasure out of it, in spite of the early hour. All that Dan could think was that she had cut across the northern outskirts of town and joined Vance as he reached the trail, to give him a send-off of sorts.

Without seeming to, Dan's team and the approaching riding horse all slackened their pace as the rider converged with the wagon. After getting over his initial shock, Dan submitted Della to a close scrutiny while she was still some yards away.

Under the stress of her recent bereavement there was still no denying her blonde beauty. The dark smudges under her eyes which signified lack of sleep merely matured her expression. She had on a black felt hat with the brim pinned up at one side. Most of her hair was tucked up inside it, and to make sure that it did not fly off, she had fixed it with a strap under her chin.

Her expression altered when she recognised the drab outlines of the prison vehicle and the rather set expression of the driver. She reined in rather sharply and favoured Dan with a somewhat mocking smile.

'Well, howdy, Dan. So it's you on the trail again, an' this time fixin' to look after three outlaws, after they're dead. It sure must be good practice for you, that sort of work. At least they can't escape if you come over drowsy an' lose control.'

Touched on the raw by her tone, Dan stiffened and retaliated. 'My, my, you do have a pleasant way of talkin', Miss Della. Anybody would know you jest had to be the daughter of a renowned judge. You show all the breedin' he managed to give you an' a whole lot besides.

'May I say how touched I am that you should cut short your beauty sleep to accompany my brother part way on his journey. Sure is a sacrifice, you bountiful young lady.'

The insulting words dripped off Dan's tongue with surprising ease. He did not have time to reflect upon how they had formed themselves in his mind before Della started to react.

'Why, Dan Marden, I don't know why I was ever civil to you. You have the vocabulary of a — a common cowhand, an' that's for sure. An' I'm sure of another thing, too. I sure did pick the best of the two Marden boys when I preferred Vance to you. As far as I'm concerned, you're a failure, Dan, an' you're likely to stay that way, too. I'm sorry I stopped to give you the time of day.'

Her face was red and her bosom was heaving against her blouse and coat as she hauled the mare's neck around and went on past the vehicle without a backward glance. Dan toyed with the whip and leaned out sideways to see her go.

Normally, if there was only the slightest difference of opinion with Della, he felt that it was all his fault and remorse inevitably gripped him. On this occasion, the remorse was lacking. He wondered why it was and whether his attitude towards his brother's intended wife was changing in a manner subtle and unbidden.

Presently, he drove on again, his mind full of the new speculation.

★　★　★

The expected reception committee awaited the arrival of the tumbleweed wagon on a high, shrub-enclosed spot to the north-east of the junction between the Middleton track and that which formed east towards Red River.

A significant fifteen yards separated Long John Verne and his half-brother, Little Sam, from the six desperadoes who had been paid and briefed at short notice to take part in the coming attack.

Long John was concealing his restlessness by drawing fiercely on a narrow cheroot. He was a tall, lean, intense individual who moved compactly with a sort of feline grace. He wore a pale dun stetson, the brim of which was permanently at a rakish angle. His hair was a medium shade of brown. A close-trimmed moustache and chin beard of the same colour encircled his rather fleshy mouth. His bulbous eyes blinked behind the smoke as Little Sam talked in his familiar nasal twang.

'Jest the same, John, we shouldn't ought to have to be hittin' this prison wagon after that young jasper in Redrock had his orders. Our cousins ought to have been out on the day of the funeral. By this time we could have made a strike somewheres an' been over the border at least into another county.'

Long John shifted the position of his back against the tree. He sniffed and nodded. 'Sure enough the activities of that young fellow need lookin' into. We made it clear what we wanted done an' he's let us down, but we'll get him before long, have no fear. One thing is for sure, springin' our boys this way is going to be more costly for the law and order men.'

Little Sam, who was anything but small, muttered imprecations and stamped a boot on a low rock. At thirty, Sam was ten years younger than his half-brother, but this was not apparent owing to his height and bulk. He was supposed to be cleanshaven, but he never looked that way. Tufts of dark hair sprouted from his ears, and chest hair flourished where loose flesh threatened to burst the buttons from his soiled chequered shirt. His undented stetson was as shapeless as the rest of him.

Sam was about to renew his argument by raising a blunt forefinger to point at his brother, but there was an interruption. One of the hired hands was calling a message.

'Hey, Long John, your brother's

comin! He looks to be in a hurry! Maybe he's seen something!'

John was alert in an instant. 'All right, you men, stand to!'

He blinked in the direction of Little Sam and the two of them untethered their horses and stood ready to mount. Two minutes later, Jake Verne, two years older than his full brother, Little Sam, ran towards them with a rifle in one hand and a spyglass in the other. Perspiration was beading his dark straggling sideburns.

'You'll never guess, Long John!' he blurted out breathlessly.

'Do we have time for guesswork?' John queried edgily.

Jake nodded and sucked in air. 'Next to our kin, the man we most want to see is headin' right for this spot!'

Little Sam was at a loss, but John seized on the truth in a flash. 'Vance Marden? Marden is comin' here right now?'

Jake assured him that such was the case. John badgered him with further questions, in case the rider was coming close but not necessarily seeking them out. Nothing, however, would shake Jake in his conviction that Vance was coming right into their midst with a message. With an effort, the outlaws contained their patience.

During the short period of waiting, Jake fanned himself with his rounded stiff-brimmed black hat. Perspiration positively leaked from his prominent lined jowls. Like Sam, he had an excess of beer to blame for his bloated waistline.

The six hired hands gave way as Vance Marden's black gelding toiled up the narrow animal track closely followed by the pack mare. Vance flinched as he saw the feral look in most of their eyes, but he pushed on through them, knowing that his salvation lay with the more deadly men beyond. He was startled again when Long John and Jake detached themselves from supporting tree boles and Little Sam tossed his knife down into the earth just ahead of the gelding's fore hooves.

Dismounting quickly, Vance brushed himself down, nodded to each of the three in turn, and moved closer to John.

'John, I guess you were disappointed about the way things happened back there in Redrock. You'll allow I couldn't be away from the burial ground myself, so I had to pay another to open the cell for me. I chose an old acquaintance who was passin' through. A gambler.'

'You're in John's debt from way back,' Little Sam reminded him ominously. 'Now you've engaged a failure to spring our kin out of jail. John ain't pleased with you. I wouldn't be in your fancy boots.'

A mere glance showed that John's protruding eyes were bright with suppressed anger. Brother Jake murmured a few words calculated to fan the flames of the leader's ire.

'Where is this jasper who should have seen our boys out of town, an' how did they come to be returned to the cells? There's something buggin' me about this whole deal. I sure would hate to find out that you've double-crossed us, Vance, seein' as how we let you off the hook over that matter of clients' money a year ago.'

'The man engaged has slipped town. The boys were returned to cells because that was the way it had to be. As they came out of the back door of the peace office they ran into serious trouble. More trouble than they could deal with.'

'What are you tryin' to tell us, Marden?' John muttered warily.

'That your cousins, the Ferrises, are dead, along with their pardner, Jonas McGall. They were caught makin' their exit at the back by some hombre late for the funeral, some man with fast guns who jest happened along. Rod and Slim made a run for it at the back, but they were shot. I've got reason to believe that McGall was shot in the back, but I couldn't say who did that because there was no one near the office when the town marshal got back there.'

Long John was known for his extremes of feeling, but his control was better. Jake and Sam, his half-brothers, had less temper and not as much control. Jake called Vance a couple of crude names and suddenly hit him hard under the left eye.

Vance bounced backwards and kept his balance with difficulty as his slithering boots fouled a low rock behind him. He fetched up hard against a tree bole and before he was properly recovered Little Sam had grabbed him by the shoulders and slammed his head hard against the trunk, dislodging his hat.

Vance knew he had to take this treatment, but he did not want to lose his senses until he had said all of his piece. He slithered downwards and fetched up short with his knees doubled under him. As soon as he had sufficient breath, he began again, choosing his words with care.

'I don't want you to attack that

tumbleweed wagon. That's what the authorities expect. All you have in there are three coffins. You can't improve the lot of the deceased trio. They'll get a burial of sorts. On the other hand, if you want to make a strike to get some of that ill feelin' out of your system, why don't you ambush the posse of Redrock men who are keepin' well to the rear?'

Little Sam came over and stared in Vance's face as though he could not be sure whether he was hearing the truth. Jake squatted on top of a rock and regarded the newcomer through half-closed eyes. Long John started to crack his knuckles, a sure sign that he was coming to a decision of some sort.

Vance felt that Long John believed his story and that had to count for something.

'Whatever you decide to do, remember I came here when I didn't really need to. I could have been on my way out of this county an' this territory for good. I was aimin' to keep my side of a bargain made with you a year ago.'

Long John cleared his throat. 'How long before that tumbleweed wagon gets to a point opposite here on the northbound trail?'

Vance answered as well as he could.

9

Dan gave water to the horse team from a small wooden barrel which he had brought along for the purpose. He also refreshed himself while they were busy and saw to his weapons. He found himself gauging the time by the sun's progress and he thought that either the posse following him was late in catching up, or that the riders were being very successful in hiding their presence.

Inevitably, as the memory of the encounter with Della faded and the spot where the east trail forked off went by, the tension mounted up in him. He had laid himself open to intense deadly action from known outlaws who knew no mercy when they were annoyed. He thought soberly that the odds on his surviving through the day were long.

All he could do was be prepared. He studied the terrain on either hand and wondered if any ordinary travellers would in any way get mixed up with the hostile strike which he anticipated on the Middleton trail. He hoped not. Anxiety made him try to think as attackers might. The east side offered the best opportunities for visibility and preparedness and also for an onslaught with a height advantage.

His mouth dried out in spite of his having drunk a healthy draught of water quite recently. There were times when he almost wished that whatever was going to take place would begin. A family in a lightweight cart went by in the opposite direction, a youngish couple full of energy and who looked as if they were seeking for land to settle on.

Dan spoke with them, but made no effort to delay in case they became involved with his troubles. A kind of relief swept over him as the distance between them widened again and his attention was once more on what lay ahead.

He was wondering how far along the eastbound trail Vance might be when he began to feel a curious sensation. His neck hairs tingled, nerve vibrations of some kind came and went up his backbone. Was this nature telling him that he was observed, that the attack was imminent?

He took a few deep breaths and turned his head slowly this way and that, attempting to get a glimpse of anything that might suggest that man or men were studying his movements. Nothing showed. He took stock of his position. His vulnerability was evident to anyone looking on.

A sudden outburst of firing was all that was wanted. He had not taken the precaution of wearing any sort of protective clothing. At his back, the high, flat, front wall of the detention wagon protected him.

Any shots calculated to bowl him over would have to come from either side and not too far back, or from ahead of him. That much was certain.

Unless, of course, some other sort of attack was planned from the rear. In any sort of a wheeled chase, the wagon was bound to be overtaken on account of its weight and the probable lack of stamina possessed by the veteran team.

The wall at his back would be a liability if the attack came from the rear because he could not see beyond it owing to its height and width. In spite of his awareness, the sudden noise of booming guns behind him made him clench his teeth and stiffen on the worn seat.

Perhaps six rifles had fired almost simultaneously, and that could only mean that the Vernes were in action, backed up by a few extras. It became clear at once that the shooting was not directed at the tumbleweed wagon, but at something well to the rear. Dan felt it was inconceivable that the outlaws had opened up on the young folks travelling in the cart. The only other consideration was that they had somehow spotted the follow-up riders from

Redrock before they attacked the wagon. *But how was that possible?*

Maybe the Vernes had more patience than the local peace officers credited them with. Dan breathed a little more easily as several more rifles went into action, this time from the level of the trail. The sounds of discharged guns mounted and redoubled until the staccato cacophony of sound gave the impression of a pitched battle of sorts being fought.

And still there was no sign of anyone approaching the detention wagon. Dan wondered seriously what he ought to do. Clearly, the action had not developed the way he expected. His allies were on the trail, and the further he drew ahead the more out of touch he would be with them.

Only two or three minutes went by while he thought over the situation. His conclusion was never in doubt. He would have to make another stop. So he slowed his team and started to look around once more. As the horses were permitted to slow their gait, Dan mopped himself down and again pondered upon his own fate.

★ ★ ★

Some three hundred yards further on, he found a rough half-circle of yellowing grass opening out on his left near a slight bend in the trail. Trees which gave access to a narrow triangle of timber hedged the open space on two sides.

Without hesitation, Dan turned off the regular track and crossed the sun-dried patch, heading for the trees. He entered them without hesitation, feeling more at ease as the foliage offered him shelter of sorts. On any other occasion with a heavy wagon he would have entered the stand warily, in case it was difficult to get the bulky conveyance out again. Now, however, with no humans other than himself, he drove in without caring, surprising himself in his lack of regard for the county vehicle.

Behind him, and seemingly at the same spot where it had started, the shooting contest between the two resolute teams of gunmen went on. Every now and again there was a short lull, as if someone had called a truce. But the lulls were short-lived and the firing was suddenly recommenced with renewed fury.

Now and again a man's hoarse voice was heard calling out. From Dan's knowledge of the affair, nothing could be told about the outcome. He had volunteered for the lion's share of the work and risk and, for his pains, he was nothing more than a reserve.

Nevertheless, he was cautious. He knew that if the shoot-out went against the Redrock men he would not have to wait too long for company. He missed his dun horse, but he had with him most of the items that he carried on trail. Along with his weapons, a water canteen, a spyglass and other items, he took with him a lariat, a tool which he had learned to use in his cow-punching days farther west.

Screened by two dwarf pines, he went to earth and waited. No more than five minutes went by before his patience was rewarded. A solitary rider showed briefly from time to time coming down the slope on the east side, above trail level. Sometimes he was hidden by rock and at other times stunted shrubs and miniature trees shrouded his progress, but it was clear that he was aiming for trail level and almost certain that his interest was in the wagon.

Dan studied him through the glass. He was not familiar with any recent photographs of the Verne gang, but one or two peace officers whose territory lay farther west than Big Springs County had at times given him a verbal description.

If this was one of them, he decided, it could only be Little Sam, the youngest of the deadly trio: the one who was deceptively overweight and apparently slow. The youngest and the heaviest. The horse which the newcomer forked was a stocky bay gelding which carried his bulk with surprising ease.

Five yards up from the trail, the rider reined in and took a good look around. He was soon satisfied with the deserted state of the track and also assured that he knew where to find the wagon, even though it had left the trail. The deep ruts left by the strong wheels indicated quite clearly where the vehicle had gone off.

Little Sam Verne rode into the trees, slowing his mount as the need for greater vigilance grew. Presently, he stopped the bay altogether as the rear of the wagon showed with its barred grille. His senses were fully on the alert, and yet he could detect no sound to suggest a human on the move; which augured ill for him.

From near somnolence in the saddle, he suddenly sprang to the ground with a revolver in each fist. Startled by the sudden move, the gelding catfooted sideways and then trotted away. Little Sam dropped to knee level and kept his senses alert for an attack he felt was bound to come.

Some ten or fifteen pregnant seconds elapsed before the sound he awaited filtered through to his ears. At once he turned around in the general direction of it. Unfortunately for him it was made by a pebble, tossed by Dan from behind a tree. No sooner had the pebble landed than the town marshal's lariat snaked out towards the gunman from the opposite direction and dropped neatly over the shaggy head topped by the undented stetson.

Sam cursed briefly as he realised that he had been tricked. He started to turn around, but the loop was speedily pulled taut so that it gripped his upper arms and partially pinned them to his chest as he sought to bring up his weapons and take aim.

Dan stepped clear of his screening tree. He had the end of the lariat wrapped round one forearm and the free hand held a Colt.

'If it's all the same to you, *amigo*, I'd

jest as soon not shoot you dead. The county already has three travellers with wooden jackets on in the wagon!'

He had attempted rather perversely to make his threat sound less than formidable, but Little Sam was not taken in. The latter spat in his direction before dropping his weapons, one after the other. Swaying slightly, the outlaw rose to his feet and Dan went towards him, hauling in on the lariat as he did so.

He had made a capture this time. A live one, and yet he did not feel any particular triumph. There were too many uncertainties about this day's events and the day, in fact, was far from finished. When they were five yards apart and the hirsute outlaw was muttering imprecations and flashing his bloodshot eyes, Dan started to assume his authority.

'Turn around and move to that tree bole on your left. I'm goin' to slacken the lariat around your chest, provided you don't do anything foolish. In case you fancy your chances I can still see Judge Lacey's expression as he died. Don't presume you won't get shot, if you ask for it.'

A short flurry of gunshots caused a slight delay before Sam made his move, but the firing was seemingly just as far away. The prisoner's shoulders slumped a little as he made the required move and placed himself with his chest towards the tree.

The uncertainty of the outcome of the greater struggle down-trail made Dan wonder for a while what he should do with his prisoner. He decided against trussing him to the tree bole and instead secured his hands and ankles with the lariat. The tying was in such a way as to keep Verne's knees bent all the time.

'You knew the men in that wagon were dead before you came along here. Who tipped you off, Verne?'

For the first time, Little Sam showed some slight enjoyment of the situation. 'Now wouldn't you like to know, lawman? An' you sure would get a surprise if you knew the truth! You may have three hombres in there ready for plantin' an' me temporarily out of action, but this little contest has a long way to go yet. So don't waste time talkin', huh?'

Dan backed off and a minute later he was out on the trail using his senses and his glass to try and assess whether he would have visitors quite soon and, more to the point, whether they would be friendly or hostile. From the trail, the shooting seemed to be farther away: as if the attackers had shifted their position and drawn the riders after them.

Dan decided not to assume anything. He returned to his live charge and after placing him in the wagon with the three occupied boxes, he saw to the horse team and backed the vehicle out of the trees and on to the trail. For a time, at least, he saw it as his duty to press on towards the county seat.

* * *

Twenty riders in all had followed up the tumbleweed wagon in an effort to get to grips with the outlaw gang. Some thirty minutes after Dan Marden had started north again with his live prisoner, Deputy Malloy, Arkensaw, the driver, and half-a-dozen other riders were hidden in trees about fifty yards back from a shallow stream to the east of the outlaws' original strike position.

Malloy expected the survivors of the gang to come riding out of the trees opposite towards their waiting guns, but when the riders emerged he saw rather disappointedly that he was lined up on other members of the posse. The two leading riders soon spotted them and one man called that the renegades had finally given them the slip.

In a couple of minutes, all those riders who were still actively engaged were mixing. Someone started to light a fire. Others dismounted and rocked their saddles. One or two, too tired to see to their mounts, merely hunkered down and rolled smokes.

Bronc Malloy, feeling sour about the whole arrangement, walked among them. 'Well, boys, all I can say is that Dan Marden's scheme has come unstuck. Here we are, one man dead and two wounded, an' no Vernes to take away as prisoners. I thought it was a foolish plan from the start.'

Here and there a man nodded or shrugged as the ambitious deputy spread his words. He was still mouthing things to the detriment of Dan Marden when he came next to the fire and the short angular figure of Arkensaw, who had come along at the last minute for the excitement.

'Seems to me you're only tryin' to blacken the town marshal's name in his absence, Deputy. At least, we made contact with the gang an' most likely we've driven them well to the east. An' three of them dead, even if they're only small-fry outlaws, has to mean something. So let's not get too depressed. After all, there may be other casualties among the outlaws we don't know about.'

One or two tired riders rallied to the defence of their town marshal and during the hours that remained of daylight, Bronc Malloy kept himself pretty much to himself. So hard had the riders ridden after driving the Verne boys off the hill slope that it was thought to be unwise to try any further pursuit before the following dawn.

As for Dan, they hoped that he would be well on his way towards the county seat, and unimpeded by enemies.

10

It was between two and three o'clock in the morning that Dan Marden had the first intimation that he was about to have company. He stretched out on the roof of the tumbleweed wagon, felt for the weapons which he had beside him, and tightened his waist belt another notch. The approach of the outlaw gang was overdue.

After taking Little Sam into custody, Dan had moved the wagon slowly farther north until the evening was well advanced. He had been disappointed that no one had overtaken him from the direction of Redrock, and the few travellers who had passed him going the other way had not lingered, knowing the nature of his vehicle and guessing at his business.

Between eight and nine o'clock he had to accept that his friends were unlikely to overtake him before dark. That being the case, he had to plan for a night on the defensive. Once again, he had drawn the heavy vehicle off the track on flat ground broken up by scattered trees and this time adjacent to a small stream.

He had spent some time in debating with himself what would be the best spot to park the wagon and, finally, he had come up with what he thought was a good idea. He had parked it in a relatively open space, except for one rather high, mature tree which was widespread and carrying a lot of foliage.

The wagon was under a spread of the tree. The lowest branch on that side closely overhung the roof and so went a long way towards camouflaging the upper part of the wagon and hiding the man stretched out upon it.

Freshly alerted from sleep, Dan yawned and then listened hard for further movement. On one hand, a twig snapped. In another direction a man rendered dry by trail dust cleared his throat. Clearly, there were several men in the vicinity and they were approaching from all sides. He was about to be ringed.

Not a pleasant prospect, having to tangle with irate outlaws who had spent several hours fighting with a town posse after learning that their kin were dead. He wondered again fleetingly how they had become aware of the deaths of the Ferrises and McGall. And then his mind was back to the present again.

He thought of the number of hours which separated him from daylight and the number of miles between himself and the nearest help. Down below him, stretched out upon a blanket between the coffins of his kin, Little Sam was still, if not sleeping.

Dan had been very cautious with his one live capture. Sam's ankle and wrist bonds had been slackened so as to permit him to sleep without excessive irritation, but a light gag had been placed across his mouth to prevent his exercising his lungs in a tight situation.

The pale moonlight did little to light up the night sky, but after a time a natural improvement in Dan's night vision showed him that two men were approaching from the east. Instinct told him that this pair were the key to the stealthy approach and that the others, coming from various directions, were unlikely to make contact first.

Five minutes dragged while the ring of attackers closed in. Dan's fire, now a heap of smoking embers some ten yards away, threw fleeting occasional flickers skyward, distorting the contours of the tufted stretch of meadow.

If Little Sam was aware of the coming confrontation, he did nothing to show it. Eventually, there was a click of a rifle lever. Dan felt that it had been done deliberately, rather than carelessly, and he gave his attention to the pair he had first spotted.

'This is Long John Verne callin' to Marshal Marden of Redrock! I know you're there an' that you're on the alert, so there's no point in pretendin' otherwise. My men are all in good fettle an' you are ringed. Do you want we should talk some, or should we open up on you from all sides?'

Dan deliberately waited for nearly a minute before he answered the outlaw's cool challenge. At the moment when Long John was thinking of calling again, he cleared his throat to answer.

'I see you, Long John, an' I have you full in my sights. If you want, we could talk briefly before I do any squeezin'. What do we have to talk about?'

'About my half-brother, Little Sam. I figure you have him there on account of we recognised his horse over towards the stream.'

'I have Little Sam with me, Long John, an' the way I see things, Sam is one good reason why you won't have your boys pepper this vehicle with careless shootin'. Otherwise there'll be four dead bodies around here instead of three. So, what else is there to say?'

Dan wondered who the fellow was beside the outlaw leader, but he had other things to think about. John's voice had developed a slight edge when he spoke again.

'You're assumin' that I think Little Sam is alive, ain't you? Well, we've seen nothin' to assure us on that point, mister. An' if you think you're simply goin' to pull that trigger on me, you'd better take a closer look at the man who is beside me. Can you see him?'

Dan's heart thumped a little faster. This last statement had to mean that Long John had a trump card of some sort to play. The person in question rose to a kneeling position, and then finally stood up.

'You know who this is, Marden?' John went on.

Dan's eyes were as good as those of anyone else in the camp area. Although the visibility was not very good he had an instinct for the profiles of people he knew. This silhouette made his heart lurch momentarily. He felt certain that he was seeing Vance; that in some way his brother had been jumped for the money he had on him.

To gain time, Dan asked: 'Who is it, Verne? This is a strange time for introductions.'

Around the hidden ring two men laughed derisively from different sides. John enjoyed a dry chuckle himself before confirming the mystery man's identity.

'This is your brother, Vance. If anything happens to me in a hurry, Vance gets it at once. Is that understood? Now, give me proof that Little Sam is alive!'

Dan's temples were throbbing as he thought over the new situation. He thought that the confrontation was difficult enough from his point of view without his kid brother becoming involved. His mind clutched at straws, but he remained cautious.

He called: 'Hey, you down there! Little Sam! Your big brother John is callin' on us! If you can hear me, kick the woodwork so he can be sure you're alive!'

Sam obliged quite promptly and before Long John could comment upon the heavy way in which the hidden man was kicking the baseboard, the town marshal had more to say.

'Don't ask for him to call out because I put a gag across his mouth to stop anything like that. You have a bargainin' point, Verne, in my brother. I'm goin' to suggest that you send Vance forward, that he cuts Sam loose.

'Sam is free to accompany you an' take his horse on this occasion provided that Vance is not molested in any way. Now, what do you say?'

Dan was breathing deeply and wondering if his suggestion had a chance of being taken up.

'If we allow Vance to join you, he could take up weapons against us an' some of us might get hurt before we lay our hands on Sam. Why don't you get down into the wagon an' free your live prisoner yourself?'

'Too risky,' Dan called back, acting out his bluff. 'I'm fond of my brother, but I could still shoot you an' get Little Sam below me, if anyone blasted Vance in a hurry!'

This time Verne allowed the silence to grow for over a minute. Dan's eyes were watering through staring fixedly along his Winchester at Long John's head.

'All right, Marden, I agree! But there'll be other days an' you mustn't expect any special sort of treatment after this. You understand? This county has not heard the last of the Verne gang an' you could be high on our list for an early death. Come to think of it, I ain't sure that you didn't kill my kin in those coffins yourself. You wouldn't like to make a statement on that, would you?'

'No, I wouldn't,' Dan argued bluntly. 'So let's see my brother movin' forward! My finger is gettin' a little shaky on this trigger, an' that's for sure. At this hour of the mornin' accidents can happen!'

There were whispered exchanges between Vance and the outlaw leader before the former started to walk forward with his hands held at shoulder level and his arms well spread.

'Move to the back door of the wagon, Vance.'

'I hear you, brother. Keep on the alert, I can wait a minute.'

'I intend to keep on the alert all the time, kid, so listen carefully. I'm goin' to toss a key down to you, one which will open the door. Also a knife, so keep your eyes skinned. Understand?'

Vance came to a halt out of sight from the roof and in a useful position. Clearly, an enemy in that position would have been well placed for a sneak attack. Dan felt good on account of his brother being that close. He was getting used now to having him around, after the initial shock.

Many listening ears heard the key on its ring hit the ground at Vance's feet. The latter shifted his position rather hurriedly as the knife followed. Dan warned him to make sure that Sam did not jump him, but the warning was unnecessary. A match flared in the dim interior of the wagon and in a surprisingly short space of time the hirsute outlaw stepped out of the back door and dropped to the level of the surrounding earth.

'All right, so your brother is out of the wagon an' free to walk away, John. Have him collect his horse from nearer the stream and then withdraw your boys.'

Long John whistled in a special way and at once the ring began to withdraw. One man met up with Sam and conducted him in his search for his horse. Vance took the precaution of stepping back into the wagon, in case anyone took a few snapshots at him before they pulled out.

To Dan's surprise, the Verne outfit pulled out with a total lack of fuss. Five minutes later, they might never have been there. He lowered himself down to the ground and warmly gripped his brother by the shoulders.

Vance murmured in his ear: 'This

sure has been a tricky day, Dan. I never did think that we'd both be in a situation like this in the early hours of a new mornin'.'

'Neither did I, but we sure do have reason to be thankful. Do you know anything about that pitched battle they had with the posse back there?'

Vance shrugged as they parted. 'Not a lot, Dan. After they jumped me up the east trail, they hid me for a while. Later, there was a lot of comin' and goin' on horseback. The Vernes had one or two casualties and so did the Redrock men, I fancy. But the outlaws shook off the posse and probably gave them the impression that they had turned east.'

Dan yawned. 'Me, after all that excitement, I'd like to take a bathe in the stream. How would you like to keep watch for a few minutes, *amigo*?'

Vance agreed readily enough and when Dan emerged again his lookout came walking back towards the bank leading his regular riding horse, the black gelding, followed at the rear by the bay mare pack horse on a long lead rope.

'Ain't this a stroke of luck, Dan? The Vernes didn't bother to look for my ridin' outfit when they wandered away from the other cayuses. I think I ought to take a bathe now, jest to celebrate.'

Vance entered the water in his underwear, and Dan, who thought that the outlaws had been altogether too casual in leaving two horses for the use of their enemies, felt himself drawn towards his brother's discarded clothes.

The most significant item was Vance's dark tailored jacket. It had built into it a secret pocket in the lining of the back. Dan knew from the first touch that the wad of bills still in there was the five hundred dollars which his brother had received from March, the lawyer, as laid down in Judge Lacey's will.

Now there was a thing. A bunch of desperate outlaws grab a man, perhaps as a hostage, and they forget to go through his pockets in search of his money. How careless could a bunch like

161

the Vernes really be?

And now Vance was back, free again, with his two quadrupeds as well as his substantial funds. In spite of himself, Dan began to wonder if Vance had not bought his freedom by selling information, or something like that. Was it a form of treachery to think ill of one's brother, one's only living kin?

Dan vigorously dried himself down and began to rig his blanket for sleeping. As his brother came back dripping from the stream, the town marshal was reminded of that formidable swelling under Vance's left eye. Someone had certainly struck him hard. He had not had it all his own way while the outlaws had him in their clutches.

11

The gentle sounds of awakening nature aroused the brothers both around the same time. For several minutes they remained propped on their rolls contemplating one another and the rugged scenery on all sides. The grey-painted battered prison wagon seemed out of place in the vastness of the landscape and, but for its presence, it would not have been difficult to dismiss the violent clashes of the day before as imaginative fantasies or dreams.

Dan stirred first, springing to his feet and tightening his belt. He collected firewood and boosted the flagging blaze so that they could take a meal before they moved on again. The bacon and biscuits tasted good and for a time they were silent, simply attending to the needs of the inner man and thinking things over.

It was anybody's guess where the outlaws had headed for, or so thought Dan as he contemplated his moves for the day. His instinct told him that he would not have any further troubles with the Vernes during the time he was in charge of the wagon and its inert contents.

His mind switched to Vance and the latter's journeyings. Dan still thought it best for his brother to head steadily east, rather than make a detour into the county seat. He said as much and Vance appeared to take his repeated advice philosophically.

Examining his last rasher of bacon, the younger man said: 'It's no use you worryin' about me, brother, I'm old enough to take care of myself. You're the one with the mission in life. Here's hopin' you'll stay as lucky after I've gone on my way.'

Dan gave a wry grin. 'Vance, I tend to forget that you have visited all the towns in this area on matters of legal business for your firm. An' I can't forget that I'm jest a couple of years older, either. Still, I figure my advice remains good. Saddler's Ford is the town to head for first. It's in the right direction, an' when you get there you can decide whether you want to make use of the stagecoach for a day or two before goin' on by railroad.

'I wouldn't use the main trail, though. I'd use a secondary track which loops a little north of the main one, so as to give the Vernes the slip if they're still in the area. You know what I mean?'

'I know what you mean, Dan. Keep out of sight for a day or two. Maybe only travel at night. That sort of thing.'

Clearly Vance was in complete agreement about his future movements. If he had any doubts about how things would turn out he kept them to himself, and Dan, with a head full of half-formed suspicions about his brother, began to look on the bright side again. He was quietly optimistic about his and Vance's travels by the time they had the veteran horse team in the shafts and ready to pull away.

An hour later a swaying signboard indicated where the Saddler's Ford trail turned off. There, they paused.

'The diversion I'm suggestin' you use is about a mile an' a half up there on the north side. It's narrow in places for wheeled vehicles and the fierce grades helped to push most Red River traffic on to the other route. How long do you think it will take for you to get to your law school in Tennessee?'

At this question, Vance laughed heartily. 'Shucks, Dan, this is the longest journey I've ever made. It's likely to depend upon the type of transport an' whether the west is friendly or not. Who can tell to within seven days?'

Dan brushed aside a slight feeling of envy for Vance and hastened on the moment of parting. Five minutes were sufficient to bring the younger Marden to a turn in the trail. After waving his

Stetson, Dan coaxed the horse team into a further effort and the creaking wagon moved north.

* * *

Telegraph messages must have reached the county seat a short time before Dan began his assault on the last mile of the journey during that evening. As a result, Sheriff Fred Inger and his deputy, Richy Furlow, were just mounting up outside the former's office as the tumbleweed wagon began to make its approach from the south.

A small crowd gathered as the vehicle moved slowly up to the front of the office, flanked by the two local peace officers.

'Give way, folks. Make room for the wagon. If you're curious I can tell you that the prisoners inside there are already in their coffins, so there'll be no spectacular transfer to our cells.'

At first, the townsfolk seemed not to believe the sheriff's frank statement, but when the driver and the two peace officers prepared to go into the office and no sound came from the wagon's interior, they were convinced. No one sent for the undertaker, but a messenger left the office to seek out the cemetery keeper.

A three-cornered conversation began with the newcomer and the sheriff seated and Deputy Farlow in a neutral standing position in front of the window. Dan drew hard on a cigarette.

'Dan, I sure am sorry my boys didn't have any success after the judge was jumped by Coyote Ridge. In fact this office has come in for a lot of criticism ever since. I don't know what the locals will think about three outlaws arrivin' here as victims of lead poisonin'. Would you care to tell me about it?'

Inger was a stocky, capable peace officer in his fiftieth year. His very fair hair and pink complexion denied his years, but the eroded grey eyes, spreading waistline and slow methodical movements told a different story. He listened well while Dan outlined the events in town on the day of the judge's funeral.

Richy Furlow, a man of over six feet in height who was almost incredibly lean, pottered about with the makings of coffee. He was almost thirty years of age although his shoulder stoop and the deceptive wide-mouthed, gap-toothed grin made him look older.

'You say some person unknown shot Jonas McGall in the back as he slipped out of jail at the rear? Did you never find out who did that, or why it was done?'

Dan sniffed and shook his head. 'It's my belief that someone passin' through was given the job of liberatin' the trio. When this fellow, whoever he was, discovered that the whole affair was goin' against him, he despatched the last man himself an' made a stealthy getaway.

'In keepin' the triple deaths a secret I thought we might draw the more formidable members of the gang out into the open.'

'According to our telegraph message, you succeeded in that, too,' Furlow put in with a throaty chuckle.

Inger whistled quietly through the smoke of his cigar and found himself wishing that Dan Marden was his man instead of Furlow.

'That's so,' Dan admitted thoughtfully. 'There were two clashes on the way here. The first one scarcely affected me at all, although I managed to make a capture. The second one, though, happened in the night an' I'm not sure that anyone would call it a victory. I lost the advantage gained earlier on.'

After taking a drink of coffee, Dan proceeded to explain his conclusions. A man who knocked on the office door for information was sent on his way somewhat impatiently by the deputy and the discourse then proceeded uninterrupted for a half-hour.

At the end, the three men sat and rocked in their chairs under a high cloud of tobacco smoke which swirled and eddied towards the grille in the rear corridor door.

'Dan, it's a pity you had to lose Little Sam Verne the way you did, but any one of us in similar circumstances would have done the same. A man doesn't hazard his brother's life for the sake of scum like the Vernes. Tell me, did you have any feelings about the reward money due for apprehendin' the dead men?'

Dan was mildly surprised. 'Are you sayin' that reward notices are already out for the three dead men?'

Inger grinned slowly. 'Well, no. Not exactly, but there's a lot of feelin' against the Verne outlaws in this town. I was thinkin' that a few dollars might be drummed up now that three of them are out of the way for good.'

'Don't bother your head about such things, Fred,' Dan replied calmly. 'On the other hand, notices ought to be put out for the rest of the gang since they've openly attacked a posse of riders and actually killed one man.'

Inger promised to put pressure on the authorities in town to offer the rewards and have the notices posted. He then stood up and looked over his guest.

'You'll be wantin' to get back to Redrock without delay, Dan, so I won't keep you any longer tonight.'

Dan stood up readily enough, but his words came as a surprise to the two local men. 'If you're thinkin' about the election comin' up in Redrock this week, don't bother, Fred. I don't intend to put up for another term as marshal.

'You see, I reckon that I'm at a turnin' point in my career. Personal affairs and certain pressin' responsibilities will have to come before the town of Redrock for a while.'

When Dan left them, shortly afterwards, his first call was at the telegraph office, where he sent a message to Redrock informing certain officials of his decision to relinquish his office and not to return for a while.

Arkensaw, a thoroughly restless individual at the best of times, sprang a
surprise on Dan when he arrived in the
county seat towards noon on the
following day. He had ridden a small
wiry horse with plenty of bottom,
borrowed from a livery in Redrock. And
trotting behind him all the way had
been Dan's own horse, his powerful
big-boned dun with the black mane and
tail.

The regular prison wagon driver
turned up outside a livery at the time
when Dan was looking over some
riding stock with a view to buying
one or having one out on hire. At
once the liveryman freed him of all
obligation and took the two trail-hot
horses into his care while their riders
went off in search of liquid
nourishment.

Dan bought the whisky. 'It sure was a
good idea of yours to bring my horse
along, Arkensaw, especially as I don't

173

intend to return to Redrock straight away.'

'I figured you might have something like that in mind, young fellow.'

Arkensaw swallowed about two fingers of the strong liquor and smacked his lips before resuming the conversation. In quiet, intimate tones he told how things had been in Redrock since Dan left, and supplied some of the details about the gun clashes with outlaws which Dan had heard a lot of but not seen.

Dan, in his turn, explained about Vance's part in the exchange when Little Sam Verne had had to be freed.

'I don't mind tellin' you, in confidence, Arkensaw, that Vance becomin' involved has worried me quite a bit. You see, the outlaws never attempted to hit the tumbleweed wagon first. They simply waited for the following posse and started to shoot down on the riders as soon as they appeared.

'Now, that has to mean something. Hittin' the rear-guard when nobody is

174

supposed to know there is one. An' when Little Sam came sneakin' up to the wagon it was clear that he knew his cousins were dead inside it.

'Somebody had to tell those boys what was goin' on, and the most likely fellow would appear to be *my* brother. Later, when there's an exchange, the Vernes leave him with his riding horses an' fail to take his travellin' money away from him. There's something smells about this whole affair.'

Arkensaw was diplomatic enough to keep quiet for a while. He poured two more shots of whisky and was well into his drink by the time he spoke again.

'It is possible that Vance might have told them that the prisoners were dead so as to prevent them from shootin' you off the box. I suppose you've thought of that?'

Dan nodded. 'I jest hope that he didn't suggest that they should shoot up the followin' riders, though. I couldn't excuse him for that. I began to have my suspicions about him before we parted, but he had a badly swollen eye which could only have been done by a punch, so I'm inclined to believe that if they put pressure on him that he didn't give in too easily.'

The older man oozed sympathy. 'You say you're not goin' back to Redrock. Have you any special ideas about where to ride next?'

'In the best interests of the judge, now deceased, and the county an' myself, I'm goin' on the hunt. Vance is headed for Saddler's Ford. I know jest how far it is an' the route he ought to be takin'. So I'm goin' lookin' for my brother. If the Vernes seek him out, I'll contact them again. If they don't, I might jest learn a lot more about Vance.'

There was another alternative and Arkensaw mentioned it before they left. 'You have my good wishes, an' I only hope that Vance ain't disappeared altogether.'

12

Two days later Dan was in Saddler's Ford. By ten in the morning after his late-night arrival he had asked around the town and made his more pointed enquiries at the office of the local lawyer who was always in touch with Hector March's office in Redrock over some matter or another.

The lawyer in question was a few years younger than March and inclined to enjoy a short gossip with men from out of town. Dan quickly brought the subject round to Vance and that prompted the lawyer to wonder if Vance had achieved his ambition to go away to law school. Dan then brought the lawyer down to earth with talk of the Vernes and explained that he thought Vance might be in some danger.

At this point the fellow's legal brain was working hard as he strode up and down the sidewalk in front of his office. From time to time, the pacing stopped and Bellows, the lawyer, looked Dan straight in the face. Dan had a feeling that was how the man would behave in a court room. He waited patiently for some sort of explanation.

'I can see that you're perturbed, Mr Marden, so I'll make my suggestion an' you can act on it or otherwise, as you think fit. Your brother was always a perfectly normal young man. At times, I thought, he spent a little more time between towns than his assignments for Mr March warranted.

'He was on full expenses and who could blame him if he took a little time off now and again to visit a lady friend?'

'You think he might have gone visitin' a lady friend in this area, Mr Bellows?'

This possibility had never even occurred to Dan. He had thought that Della Lacey back in Redrock was the only young woman in Vance's life. His eyes clouded with speculation. The lawyer checked his impatience and waited.

He coughed. 'Just because Vance is not where you expected to find him doesn't mean that he's in trouble, er, Dan. I was just thinking that a visit to a small ranch a few miles south of here might give you a surprise.'

Dan thanked his informant and asked for more details, but Abe Bellows claimed he knew no more than just the vague idea that the ranch with the eligible girl lay south of Saddler's Ford and west of the direct trail to Eastberg, the only other town in that district.

By noon, he had failed to gather any further information and so he set off on the short ride south, scorning for once the idea of resting up during the hottest part of the day. A rather wild-looking prospector told him that the Barre outfit was the only one in the area, and it was clear by his manner that he did not really think of it as a going concern.

Around two in the afternoon, he saw his first glimpse of the ranch from a rounded hill top and used his glass to bring it up closer. The house was a shallow-roofed log cabin with the minimum number of buildings around it and only a small herd in the yellowing range grass beyond.

His approach to the spread was through dense timber, and while he was still in the shadow there was a commotion around the buildings which suggested serious trouble. The voice of an elderly man, sounding more like a croak than an angry shout, protested at something, and a younger man laughed sneeringly.

Dan pushed the dun as a young woman's voice, sounding very perturbed, protested even louder.

'Doggone it, Pete, you Rhode boys ought to be able to keep that fool dog of yours out of the meadow! Didn't you learn anything when your Pa brought you up in the mountains? I don't know why I keep you, so help me, I don't!'

'You keep us, Miss Millie, 'cause you have to! Ain't nobody else wants to work on the M Bar ranch, so you're stuck with us! Ain't my fault if Job's dog escapes from the bunkhouse every once in a while now, is it?'

The fretful yapping of the dog grew a little fainter and was soon partially drowned in the bawling of cattle. Dan, on the dun, came out of the timber at speed. The sun squint matured his expression as he took in the sight before him. There was a pole corral to the right of the buildings. Two homely-looking men in faded overalls were sitting on the top rail and grinning disinterestedly at the milling cattle in the background, some forty in number.

As Dan watched the racing dog cut them into frightened groups and started the inevitable stampede. A tall distracted young woman, dressed in a white peasant blouse and denims, ran to the corral to run out a pinto pony, while an elderly man who must have been in his sixties swayed on creaking legs between the house and the blacksmith's shop, gripped by old age and indecision.

Dan hesitated and then followed the girl. He overtook her before she reached the corral, and in spite of the swiftly developing situation he found himself admiring her. The girl in question must have been about twenty-three years old. Her long straight brown hair was parted in the middle and brushed back and tied at the nape of her neck. The blouse and denims showed off a nice shapely figure, temporarily exaggerated because she was breathing hard.

She ignored him until she was up with the poles, and then she had to rest against them to get her breath back. Dan glared at the overalled couple whose dog, seemingly, was the cause of the trouble. They were very slowly getting down off the top rail.

'Sure, sure, I'm Millie Barre, the owner of this so-called outfit, mister, but I have all the trouble I can handle at the moment an' visitors are not welcome.'

Dan touched his hat and turned the prancing dun. 'I came here especially to make certain enquiries, but I could help, given the slightest encouragement.'

Her shrewd eyes picked out the darker patch on the breast of his shirt where his star had been pinned until recently.

'You don't look like a cowpuncher to me, but if you want to, you could help to head off that herd of forty before they reach Foamin' Creek further south. They're all I have . . .'

Her voice tailed off and suddenly Dan knew that he had to help her. The smell of the dust put up by the receding cattle and the challenge of the stampede put him on his mettle.

'All right, I'll have a go,' he promised.

Next, he turned his attention to the homely brothers who were eyeing him malevolently. 'Get some ridin' horses an' follow me, you two. If I catch a glimpse of that mangy dog of yours clear of the herd I'll shoot it stone dead, so help me!'

And then he was rounding the pole corral and extending the dun to a useful gallop across the sun-dried meadow. He was keen on what he was about to do and never once did he look back. Those who were left behind heard a single revolver shot some five minutes later, and the scarcely helpful Rhode brothers thought he had carried out his threat to kill their dog. A search some little time later revealed that it had merely been creased with an accurate shot across its back.

★ ★ ★

Dan's first working job with cattle in a long time carried with it a certain amount of luck. In the first place, all the groups went in the same general direction, and secondly the sudden noisy scuttling of some beast the size of a wild pig sent the leading animals into a small park entirely surrounded by a ring of rocks. The entrance to the park was the only exit. Animals in the rear pushed in upon the leaders and by the time the packed milling had tired them they were reluctant to rush out again and continue their precipitate course towards the remote waterway known as Foaming Creek.

Dan rested his dun and did a few minutes of tuneful whistling before he attempted to break out the first group. There were a critical few minutes before the bulk of the thirsty creatures began to meander back again. Ten minutes later, the Rhode brothers arrived, and showed by their easily read faces that they were surprised to find that the stranger had succeeded so well and so quickly.

'All right, you boys, take over,' Dan instructed brusquely. 'I reckon you owe that young female a few favours, so make sure you can get back without too long a delay.'

Pete Rhode, the older of the two

brothers, had a sharp retort upon his tongue, but by the time he had thought out exactly what he wanted to say, Dan had turned his dun and was already moving away.

★　★　★

Millie Barre, who had decided against riding after the cattle herself, was even more surprised when Dan came riding back to the house and hitched his horse to the rail.

He grinned and touched his hat. 'I had a bit of luck, miss. The leadin' bunch ran into a park. That way I was able to overtake them. Your lazy brothers are bringin' them back now. I wonder if I've earned a drink, and maybe the answers to a few questions?'

Sighing with relief, Millie Barre favoured him with a smile which transformed her small, regular features. 'Why, sure, mister. Come right on in an' take the weight offen your feet. I'll get you a drink of fruit juice to slake your thirst. After that, you can take coffee if you want. I sure am obliged to you for what you've done. An' me thinkin' you'd never handled cattle before.'

In the low-ceilinged parlour, Dan drank almost a pint of fruit juice, and Millie seated herself at the back of the table after calling to her old retainer to take care of the dun horse.

'Miss Millie, I'm lookin' for a young man who rode out in this direction. I'm not sure if he's in trouble or not. I wondered if you could help me. My name is Marden, by the way. Dan Marden.'

'Well, howdy, Dan. Glad to meet you, I'm sure. We don't get many young visitors in these parts, but if you could describe this young man it might mean something to me.'

Having said this, the girl dropped her gaze to the table top as though some unbidden thought had troubled her. Ignoring this reaction, Dan began to conjure up the words to describe his brother.

'This young fellow is a couple of years younger than I am. Rounder in the face, sandy-haired and freckled. He's usually clean-shaven and when last seen he was wearin' a cream stetson, white shirt, black tie and a dark tailored jacket. Does that description mean anything to you?'

Obviously it had. Millie had turned pale and one thin shapely hand clutched at her throat. Her brown eyes stared unseeingly. After a few seconds, her distress began to affect Dan, who half rose to his feet and gestured towards her.

'Is anything wrong, Miss Millie?'

'What did you say his name was?'

'Name of Vance Marden and a native of Redrock. Do you think you know him? Have you seen him?'

Millie raised her shoulders rather hopelessly. She rose to her feet and collected a small piece of pasteboard which turned out to be a photograph from the lower drawer of a small bureau. 'My friend called himself Vince

Munday. A name strangely like your missin' person. Here's a picture of Vince.'

Dan moved around closer, taking the photo from her and studying it. At once he knew that he was looking at a likeness of his brother. Dan was puzzled and at the same time troubled. On the bottom of the picture Vance had written: *To Millie, with love. Vince.*

'Do I take it that this young man used to call here quite often, Miss Millie?' Dan asked carefully.

'About every other month, at one time. But he hasn't been here lately, an' I don't think he'll ever be callin' again. He used to come in my father's time, but that's well in the past now.'

Clearly, the young woman was bitter and emotionally upset.

'Judgin' by your attitude, something happened between you, Millie. I wouldn't press for more details except that he is my brother and I need to find him. If you could bring yourself to fill me in on a few more details I'd take it as a kindness.'

For a couple of minutes Millie's normally placid face was torn by conflicting emotions. Eventually, however, she made an effort to recover her composure and forced a brief smile.

'Vince had the gambling habit. I don't know if you knew this. One day he came out here to try and borrow money to cover his losses. My Pa was up the range at the time, and I told Vince that in any case Pa wouldn't consider loanin' money for that sort of thing. Vince acted like he accepted what I said and he left shortly afterwards. Pa didn't get in before dark.

'The few of us who live here retired. Someone who knew his way about slipped into the building, produced the key to the safe and helped himself to Pa's savings. I'm a sound sleeper and the intruder would have been able to slip away unnoticed if Pa hadn't happened to be returning by dark from our northern line cabin, where he'd been tendin a couple of sick calves.

'Pa arrived in time to notice the intruder makin' off, an' he checked the house, discovered the theft and at once gave chase. About a mile away from here he must have almost caught up. There was a flurry of shots and then silence. Pa's horse found its way back here, but we didn't see Pa alive any more.

'The shots must have spooked his horse. He fell into a gully and died there of his injuries. We found him halfway through the following morning. We never saw any further trace of the robber, an' Vince has not been back to this day. But I'm certain he did it.

'I went to town the followin' mornin' an' told the marshal, but no one ever found any trace of Vince or the money that was taken. So there's how it is.'

The girl stopped talking and the room was silent. Dan toyed with his hat, wondering what he could say for the best.

'I have very good reasons for wantin'

to catch up with my brother, an' I *will* do. If I find that he is responsible for this crime I'll do something about it. My conscience would demand action on my part, even though he is my kin. You see, I was a town marshal myself until jest recently.'

'I believe you, Dan,' Millie answered calmly. 'I hope you find him, for your sake. There was a place he used to go when he wanted a bit of peace. A deserted shack near a creek on the other side of the trail between Saddler's Ford an' Eastberg. Maybe you ought to look there.'

Dan peeled twenty dollars in notes from his roll and insisted upon leaving them. 'Take them and use them. I'm sure you must be short of funds. When I've seen this thing through I'll come back, if I may. If you had more hired hands could you afford to pay them?'

Millie gave an uneasy laugh. 'I might jest be able to pay one or two hands if I can sell part of the stock. But labour is not easy to get. Leastways, not in

Saddler's Ford. Somebody's put the word around that this isn't a good place for waddies.'

'If you could take a little time off and go yourself to Eastberg you might do better,' Dan suggested. 'In any case, do your best to keep goin'. If I get my present assignment out of the way I might jest come back and offer my own services. How would that be?'

The idea obviously pleased Millie. She warmed in her attitude and insisted that Dan should stay the night before going on with his search. Dan agreed. During the rest of the day he did several useful jobs around the spread, including shoeing a couple of horses.

As soon as he relaxed on his bed roll in a barn troubled thoughts assailed him. This day had seen many more suspicions mounting against Vance. The sum total of them to date made Dan wonder if Vance ever intended to go to distant Tennessee to embark upon the protracted studies necessary to become a lawyer.

13

The population of Eastberg was about one hundred less than that of its twin town, Saddler's Ford. It had fewer supporting ranches beyond its boundaries and the waterway which had been a factor counting towards its birth was for quite a stretch permanently muddy. The local ranchers had to work hard all the year round to keep going; no one became rich.

The Red River boundary with the state of Louisiana was between twenty and thirty miles of easy riding country and that was probably what kept the town from going into a decline.

Dan Marden, who arrived there after spending an extra day in the wilderness in contemplation, was indifferent to its average amenities. After all the things that he had learned about Vance, some of which had to be true, he was no longer in a hurry to overtake his younger brother. And yet he could not give up the search altogether. There was still the matter of his personal business with the Vernes. That had to be finished somehow. It was not the sort of business which could be shelved and forgotten.

At two in the afternoon, Eastberg was hot and its streets thinly populated. Dan first surrendered his horse to an ostler and quickly followed up with some beer for his thirst. He used his ears and his eyes for signs of Vance, feeling more like a private investigator rather than a worried kinsman.

A sleepy Chinese reluctantly prepared him a meal and after that he took a nap on a bench in front of a saloon which had been boarded up due to lack of business. People walking and talking in the street roused him about two hours later.

He rolled himself a cigarette and smoked it in leisurely fashion. Next, he gave himself a thorough wash under a pump and changed his shirt. Feeling much more human, he contemplated his future movements.

Eastberg was not a town which he knew well. The peace officers were strangers. So was the town's lawyer, although Dan knew his name: one Major John Hinkson, long since retired from the cavalry. A stroller told him where to find the office and he walked along the sidewalk on the north side of Main Street towards the swinging shingle which marked the premises.

Some fifty yards from the building he could see a cluster of three men standing in front of it. One of them, he felt sure, was Major Hinkson himself. Hinkson was a tall, striking figure in a dark suit with the ramrod back of a former cavalryman. He looked to be around sixty years of age. The hair which curled out from under his tall felt hat was white. His waxed and pointed moustache was grey, probably darkened by the wax.

Alongside of the lawyer was a squat

figure of a man with a hunched back. This character's full face was adorned with a flowing brown walrus moustache. Spectacles under a green eye-shade hid his eyes. He looked like a clerk in the lawyer's employ.

The source of the trio's interest was a fine long-legged palomino horse which the third man was holding by the head. Dan blinked as the horse-holder's stance surprised him. The outline and the clothing were familiar, although the head was turned away from him. Surely, this was Vance! But what was he doing showing off a costly riding horse to the Major?

Dan's pulse quickened. His pace slowed. He blinked his eyes several times, wondering if they were playing tricks on him. He stumbled over a worn board, so intense was his concentration on the small group ahead of him. Some thirty yards short of the trio, he came to a halt, resting a hip against an empty hitch rail. What did this mean? Was Vance trying to sell the beast, or was he merely showing it off to an old acquaintance?

Clearly this *was* Vance. He was talking in a rather loud voice and gesticulating with his free hand. Dan expected his brother to turn and look down the street and see him at any time, but this did not happen. It seemed almost as if Vance was talking against time.

Suddenly a dog barked in the offices behind the lawyer. The startled figure of Hinkson broke off the conversation and started towards the door. As he did so, a shot rang out and at once everything in that part of the thoroughfare was transformed.

More shots echoed around the offices. The barking of the dog was checked abruptly. Major Hinkson pulled a gun and threw open the door, but a bullet aimed at him hit him in the upper arm and threw him back again on to the sidewalk. The man with the hunched back dropped on one knee and then rolled on the boards, keeping down for safety.

Vance Marden shifted his weight this way and that, and then he was hauling the beautiful horse forward and making a leap for the saddle.

Dan called hoarsely: 'What's goin' on up there?'

Vance made the saddle, pulled his stetson more tightly over his head and forced the animal to a gallop, taking it hurriedly across the street and into an alley on the north side. No one answered Dan's query, but Major Hinkson rolled off the sidewalk to the lower dirt level. He relinquished his weapon and contented himself with gripping his grooved arm. As Dan came up, he nodded towards the front door of the office.

'Intruders in there, mister. Must be robbin' the place. I figure they shot my dog, it was sleepin' under my desk. See what you can do, but don't take any chances. I don't want your death on my conscience!'

Dan paused momentarily for breath. He sized up the situation, heard movements inside and decided that he would have to take a chance. He put a bullet through a pane of glass to one side of the door, drew several bullets from within and promptly dived through the door at a low level.

'All right, Sam, let's pull out pronto! Ain't no use in hangin' on now that pesky dog has given us away! Are you ready?'

The shouts came from the room beyond the second door. Dan had dived into a short corridor, a place used for waiting visitors who wanted an interview with the lawyer.

On impulse, Dan called: 'Hold on a minute, Long John!'

'What for?' came the edgy reply.

With a smothered oath, Little Sam Verne, Dan's one-time prisoner, opened the door nearer the street in the corridor and came at Dan from the side. In his haste he knocked over a tall hat-stand, the top of which struck Dan on the head, temporarily stunning him.

A bullet passed through the side of

his hat brim, just above the left ear, making his head sing. At the same time, Little Sam leapt over his sprawled body and dived through the second door as someone on the street fired through the main door to liven things up a little. Oddly enough, the bullet did not find a human target. Sam made his way through the rear door. He would probably have hesitated long enough to make sure Dan was dead but for the latest threat from the sidewalk.

Doors further back slammed. Dan hauled himself up as far as his knees and swayed sideways. His right hand shook a little with the .45 Colt in it as he went through the door ahead of him not knowing what was on the other side.

His head was still far from clear when he straightened up in the private office and looked around for a moving target. The main item in the room was a great leather-topped desk towards the right and under a side window. His eyes were taken by the safe with its heavy door wide open beyond the desk.

The back door of the building was through a small partitioned room containing a wash-basin and a filing cabinet. Dan had his head through the connecting door when two bullets came through the window in the rear wall of the partitioned section and had him ducking rather late for safety.

The hastiness of his movement caused his head to spin again and before he knew what was happening, he had tripped over something on the floor and measured his length again. Not, however, before his head hit the wall at the rear of the private office with a thud which the ill-used stetson on his head could only partially diminish. His senses reeled again. He had a feeling that his brains were seeping out through his ears and then he knew no more for a time.

★　★　★

A loud, raucous voice aroused him, although for a time the words uttered did not mean anything. Heavy feet came in on dusty boots and his body was straggled by more than one man. He heard the hammer of a gun click, and that helped him to think coherently at last. He rolled over rather painfully and learned for the first time what it was that he had fallen over.

It was the dead body of the Major's dog, a long-limbed black animal with a handsome head. In life, he had used it as a gun dog when he went hunting on horseback. It was capable of covering several miles through rough country.

A stocky, bandy man with brown teeth and a breath which suggested he chewed tobacco, had a suggestion to make.

'Ain't nobody else in the vicinity, Marshal. How would it be if I forced a few quick answers out of this stranger here? He ain't badly hurt!'

A high-pitched voice belonging to the local town marshal was in sharp contrast to the other. 'Seems to me the first thing you ought to do, Shorty, is to relieve him of that gun! Or are you lookin' for an excuse to shoot him while he's down?'

Before Dan could offer any sort of an explanation, the deputy put a boot on his wrist and rather brutally collected the revolver which Dan had held on to.

'Sure enough, some thievin' jaspers have emptied the Major's safe! He sure will be mad about that,' the marshal murmured.

'And about the death of his dog,' Dan added, sitting up slowly.

The swarthy deputy known as Shorty was examining the gun he had taken over. 'He's only fired one chamber, Marshal.'

Dan made an effort and succeeded in separating his aching body from that of the dog. He then removed his hat and felt around his head. Over his left ear he encountered a small fine smear of blood which recalled to his mind how close he had been to death.

The deputy was stomping around the place, probably having a close look at things which would have been denied him in ordinary times. Suddenly Dan tired of him and his officious ways.

'I take it you ain't ambitious, Deputy,' he remarked heavily.

'What's that supposed to mean, stranger?'

'I mean every time you draw breath Long John Verne and his kin are gettin' steadily further away from this office with the Major's money. Why don't you go after him?'

The marshal and his deputy, clearly surprised by the suggestion that they had narrowly missed a head-on shooting brawl with the most notorious renegades in the county, did not quite know what to make of Dan.

'How's the Major makin' out?' the latter asked, conversationally.

The deputy followed a suggestion by his superior. He went out in front to take a look. Major Hinkson, who had earlier lost consciousness, called through from the sidewalk.

'Do what you can for that fellow with

the auburn hair, marshal! I wouldn't want anything to happen to him now, if he's survived!'

The marshal, a thickset fellow with a fleshy, lined face, nodded to the suggestion without answering.

'Who are you, stranger, anyways, an' what are you doin' here at such a tricky time?'

'The name's Dan Marden. Until a few days ago I was marshal of Redrock in this county. Maybe you've heard of me over the telegraph recently. I was on the trail of unfinished business, in a manner of speaking. This isn't the first time I've clashed with the Vernes lately. Only today, I was a little on the unlucky side.'

Clearly, the local man knew Dan by repute. His bloodshot eyes registered that much.

'How do you know it was the Vernes if you were unconscious when we found you?' he asked suspiciously.

'Because I actually heard Long John call out. I answered him. If Little Sam hadn't come out of that other room things might have turned out a whole lot different.'

Dan stood up and tested himself for steadiness. The room had ceased to swing about. As he started to think over the recent precipitate happenings, the men who had found him went out of his thoughts. He was concerned about Vance again. Vance and the big palomino horse.

Who would ever believe Vance was accidentally out in front at the same time as the Vernes were breaking in at the back, and who would think Vance's presence at that time was mere coincidence?

Dan felt sure that the Vernes would make good their escape on this occasion. But would Vance come back to finish off his conversation with the Major?

Hinkson broke in upon his thoughts, calling for him to go through to the front.

14

Inevitably, a crowd gathered in front of the Hinkson law office. The lawyer ignored a lot of the folks who had only come along on account of the sensation and left his clerk, the hunch-backed Jacob Sloan, to do the talking. The only man Hinkson was specially interested in at that time was Dan Marden, and because of the welter of bodies, ordinary conversation was almost impossible.

Hinkson eventually lost patience. 'Oh, come on with me, Dan. Let's go look for some coffee, or something stronger. The doctor can come lookin' for me. He'll know where to look.'

The crowd gave way for the two men, who sauntered off down the street until they found a quiet café with a small alcove, and there they talked over a couple of small cigars.

'Were you expectin' the Vernes to

happen along today, Dan?' the lawyer asked curiously.

'Not exactly, Major. I felt they might turn up in these parts any time, however, an' so I was not surprised. My brother, Vance, is on his way to law school some distance away, an' he had previously run into the Vernes on trail. I had to exchange one of their number for Vance, otherwise he might have been in serious trouble.

'How I came to this conclusion I can't rightly remember, but I thought that somehow the outlaws might try to contact my brother again as he made his way further east in the county. So I came lookin' for him. I drew a blank in Saddler's Ford an' so I came on here.

'Could I ask you something? What was Vance tryin' to do with that fine palomino horse?'

In spite of the pain coming from his arm, John Hinkson smiled when the horse was mentioned. 'Why, what would a young fellow be doin' with a horse like that? He was showin' off its finer points, Dan. Who wouldn't? I had the impression, too, that he would sell it if a suitable figure was offered. I reckon he'd run down on his funds, been livin' it up on the way across the county.

'You ain't thinkin' he did the wrong thing in makin' off like he did, are you?'

Dan shook himself out of his rather intense concentration and tried to answer evenly. 'Well, no, I guess not, Major. Not if *you* don't think that. I suppose if he'd hung about on the offchance of tryin' to be useful his horse might have stopped a bullet in a vital spot and that would have been the end of it. Maybe he did the right thing, after all. What I'm wonderin' right now is what he is doin' an' where he is doin' it.'

'Are you afraid he might clash with the outlaws again outside of town?' Hinkson asked gently.

'It's always a possibility,' Dan admitted. 'Those Vernes pop up all over the place. Besides, if they happened to see that horse they'd have a good enough reason for searching him out. I wonder if I ought to ride out and look for him.'

Hinkson examined the butt of his cigar. He was thinking that he still had three or four good draws on it before it would have to be stubbed out. In the privacy of Dan's thoughts were other doubts about Vance which he did not intend to make known to this lawyer who still believed in him as a respectable young Westerner.

'Vance will be back when he's good an' ready, Dan, but if you can't settle I suppose you wouldn't do any harm to do a little horse ridin' on the north side of town. Mind you don't run into the Vernes yourself, of course. I mean don't clash with them unprepared.'

Given an opening, Dan took the lawyer's well-intentioned advice. They parted amicably, and Dan exchanged a word or two with the doctor, who was on his way in.

On the way to the livery stable to collect his horse, the ex-town marshal picked up what he could by way of gossip. He gathered that the wires between Eastberg and the county seat had been running hot with long exchanges about the Vernes and that Deputy Shorty Payles had taken a small posse out of town in the direction which the Vernes had gone.

No one expected the deputy and his half-a-dozen men to overtake the Vernes, but this move had been thought to be a good one, if it only succeeded in keeping the outlaws moving farther away until a bigger force of riders could get into the area from the county seat.

No one could blame the county sheriff, Fred Inger, if he seemed to be slow off the mark. The Vernes had earlier shown themselves to be very elusive.

★ ★ ★

Dan's eyes were very busy even before he walked his dun horse out of town. A palomino horse should be easy to spot, if it was back there. But why should it be?

Clearly, Lawyer Hinkson thought Vance would be back again in his own good time, but the lawyer did not know as much as Dan did about Vance's double-dealings between towns. Dan felt depressed as the dun took him up the rock-eroded dusty trail to the north.

His trained peace officer's mind, coupled with his suspicions over recent happenings, made him believe that Vance's presence in front of the office at the critical time was no accident. Dan felt almost certain that he had been sent there by design to distract the lawyer and his clerk away from the offices at the very time when the outlaws had chosen to break in.

Vance had played the part of a decoy. He had played his part well. Too well, if anything. In Dan's estimation that palomino was worth more than the price of both the other two animals which Vance had with him when he left Redrock. Maybe he had spent some of the money provided in the judge's will to buy it.

If so, he had gambled with the judge's money in the hope of making a big profit; which was scarcely the thing to do with money provided for a special purpose in a much-respected professional person's will.

The dun cleared timber and pressed on down a slight gradient. Dan occasionally glanced from side to side of the trail, but his thoughts were not really upon his search. He was brooding fitfully over his brother and his brother's affairs and no amount of effort would set his mind on anything else. At least, not for some time.

He came round to thinking that perhaps Vance had never intended really making the long trip into studious inactivity while he won his qualifications in law. Maybe he had no real intention of settling down. If that were so, how would Della Lacey be affected?

Dan reflected upon Della with a certain detached interest. He still admired her, but he now knew for certain that he had no lasting affection for her. She was pretty, attractive and very desirable, but a man did not hanker after a woman even out west unless he had some feeling for her. As far as Dan was concerned, Della was simply Jonathan B. Lacey's daughter, a young and wilful female to be protected, and that was all.

He tested out his reactions to the idea that she might never become his sister-in-law. There was a surprising lack of deep feeling and that had to mean something.

The need to negotiate a winding track though thick brush frequently loaded with sharp rocky upthrusts finally challenged his innermost thoughts and made him look outwards. He began to take more notice of the terrain and the direction in which the trail was taking him.

About a half-hour later, the going underfoot became harder. On a shelf of rock he had to slow down and when a secondary track of minor proportions loomed up on his right, there was no visible sign to suggest which direction recent traffic had taken.

Dan stopped there. He dismounted and rocked his saddle and gave the dun a hat full of water. After that, he pushed on towards the north for upwards of a mile and a half without getting the least confirmation that he was on the right track.

One thing was clear. The route which Vance had taken out of town was not one frequented by wheeled traffic. It was altogether too difficult for carts of any kind. He decided that a high point on the track was a likely place for a further halt and from there he looked around some more, using his spyglass to advantage.

The trail was practically his alone. The nearest cloud of dust put up by saddled horses coming south was more than two miles way. He slackened his rein and ascertained what he could learn from the trail-wise dun. Encouraged by him, it flicked its black tail a couple of times, turned on the semi-circle of rock on which it was standing, and clearly indicated that it was ready to go back.

Dan knew many men who would take that as a true indication of what to do next. He, however, was not entirely convinced about such things. His horse, he knew, was a clever, intelligent animal, but it had no clear idea in his opinion of what they were looking for.

He yawned, turned it about, and allowed it to start back along the same track. Within four hundred yards, he turned off to his left, striking across virgin land liberally sprinkled with spiked shrubs of divers varieties.

★   ★   ★

A slight incident with a disturbed rattler which had a bad effect upon the dun, and his own growing thirst and conviction that he was not going to locate Vance finally made Dan head back on to the main trail again and ride for Eastberg.

It was not until he was halfway back that he recalled something he had learned earlier. Millie Barre, the rancher's daughter, had said something about Vince having a hideaway somewhere east of the trail between Eastberg and Saddler's Ford. Maybe he had gone there.

Slowing a little, Dan studied the sky, the position of the sun, and thought about the points of the compass. He came to the conclusion that the ill-marked trail which he had been following did not lead to anywhere in particular within the county and that was reason enough for the lack of traffic.

As closely as he could recollect from a recent survey of a map, the direction of Saddler's Ford was to the north-west. Therefore, Vance's supposed hideout might have been to the west of the route which he had been following all the afternoon, instead of to the east, as he had thought.

He yawned a few times more and his concentration waned. He found himself studying the going down of the great orange orb of the sun far to westward. This contemplation salved his troubled mind for a while. He found himself wondering if it looked even more magnificent from the water's edge on the distant Pacific coast of California, a state in which he had once worked.

The lamps were lighted along the main thoroughfares of the town as he walked the dun back to its starting point, the main town livery. The liveryman, who kept late hours, took the horse into his care without demur, nodding to Dan's terse remarks and all the while sucking gently on a clay pipe.

Don collected his bed roll from the liveryman's care, enquired the name and whereabouts of the hotel and set off in search of it. He found it situated near the west end of the main street and was surprised to find a lamp still burning in a wall bracket in the foyer.

A mounting column of tobacco

smoke was rising from behind the counter and he was pleasantly surprised again to find a man in an ornate tasselled cap sitting on a low seat behind the counter, almost as if were waiting for custom.

'Good evenin' to you,' Dan remarked politely. 'I'm sorry to call so late, an' I didn't really expect to find anybody active at the desk. Do you usually keep such late hours?'

The clerk, a stooping man with baggy eyes and a lined face, had an interest in the business. He shrugged and moved his pipe around his worn teeth, blinking frequently as he pushed the hotel register towards the newcomer.

'Any other day in the year almost, I'd have been asleep for over an hour by this time. You're jest lucky, mister, because a rather important female visitor was expected this evenin'. In fact, she only arrived a half-hour ago.'

Dan pushed back his hat. He did not think that the woman could be anyone of his acquaintance until he saw the name at the bottom of the page in the register. And then he knew that he was due for further surprises.

'I'm Dan Marden from Redrock. I was involved in the shootin' fracas at the lawyer's office earlier on. I can't help notin' the name of this here young lady who's signed in ahead of me. As a matter of fact, she's rather more than an acquaintance. In fact, she's supposed to be marryin' my brother when the time comes.'

A dramatic change came over the face of the clerk, who had taken Dan at first for an ordinary trail rider. 'You mean you really know Miss Lacey, the late judge's daughter? Maybe you're the person she came all this way to see?'

Dan noted that the key to Della's room was no longer on the board.

He answered diplomatically. 'She didn't warn me that she was comin' all the way to Eastberg, but I certainly will be havin' talk with her come tomorrow mornin'.'

Dan moved slowly up the thinly

carpeted stairs, reflecting that Della had used the same route just a short while ago. He still found it hard to believe that she had made the long journey to Eastberg, right into the heart of the country where the trouble was.

For the life of him he could not think of anything which would have drawn her here other than an urgent message from brother Vance.

His immediate and obvious conclusions helped him to compose himself for sleep. It seemed that he had a good chance of seeing his brother again right here in this town, so the day's ride had not been wasted. Besides, although Vance was all kinds of a fool he was unlikely to bring renegades along when he kept his appointment.

15

The meeting between Dan and Della occurred in the steamy interior of the café where Dan had taken coffee with the lawyer on the previous day. The proprietor, thinking he was doing the right thing, conducted Dan personally into his curtained alcove where Della was already eating and at the same time hopefully awaiting her contact.

Dan touched his hat, had second thoughts and then removed it.

'Good day to you, Della,' he began, his face breaking into a smile.

He did not miss the look of disappointment which crossed her fresh, expectant face. She paused with a loaded fork halfway to her mouth. Eventually, her upbringing overcame her disappointment and she gestured for him to sit down at her table.

As soon as the proprietor had gone,

she turned to him. 'Dan, I didn't expect to find you here, or anywhere else on this trip for that matter. Tell me, are you in touch with Vance? Have you brought me a message from him?'

Dan hung up his hat, occupied the chair opposite and carefully adjusted his hair. He had just shaved before coming along to the café and he dearly wanted to look his best for the meeting, even if it had little significance for him.

'I was in touch with Vance yesterday, but he left town in a hurry an' I'm not quite sure how long he will be away. Did he ask you to come along here to meet him?'

Della finished chewing a mouthful of food before attempting to answer. 'I thought you said you were in touch with him yourself?'

Her counter query sounded like a challenge and Dan found himself becoming a little tense. Only the prompt arrival of his breakfast prevented a hasty retort on his part which might have prevented further healthy exchanges later on.

'Maybe you haven't heard? Yesterday the Verne outlaws attack the offices of Major Hinkson. Vance was talking to the Major at the time when the attack occurred. He left in too much of a hurry for me to talk to him. Now, will you stop fencin' and tell me the answers to a few simple questions? I am obligated to you on account of your father's last words, otherwise I wouldn't but in upon what you seem to think is your private business.'

Della coloured up. To cover the growing silence between them, Dan made inroads into his bacon and eggs. He was good and hungry, having retired the previous evening without benefit of supper, and most of the food on his plate had been consumed by the time Della had calmed herself sufficiently to resume conversation.

'I'm sorry for my earlier attitude, Dan. Vance sent for me. He sent a message which suggested he needed help in Eastberg. I was to come alone on the buckboard if I thought I could make it. And I was to wait for him here. He suggested that he had been robbed of some of the money since he left Redrock. It appears he encountered outlaws on the trail between towns. Do you have any knowledge of that?'

Dan emptied his coffee cup. 'He met with outlaws between towns, all right, Della. And what I propose to tell you, you will probably take badly seein' as how I am Vance's brother. While I've been out lookin' for him, and for the killers of your father, I've found out things.

'Reluctantly I have to tell you that Vance may not be as reliable a person as you have been led to believe. There may be incidents in his life that he wouldn't tell you, things that he wouldn't want anyone in Redrock to know about.

'If he ever shows signs of wantin' to break off his engagement to you it might be a good thing to let him go his own way.'

Della, who had reddened again, grounded her coffee cup rather hurriedly, spilling the dregs into the saucer. She fumed.

'Dan Marden, I don't rightly know what to make of you. You, who was supposed to act the part of Vance's father! Here you are runnin' him down when he isn't here to defend himself. At least, I take it that's what you're doin'. You'll be telling me next he's leadin' a double life! Am I supposed to believe that?'

Della paused for breath. Twin red patches of colour in her cheeks warned Dan that there was more to come. He made an effort to keep his own temper under control, and spoke first.

'Before you blow your stack will you tell me if you are carryin' with you a considerable amount of money?'

The girl blinked hard. 'Do you know what *I* think, Dan? I think you're jealous of your brother's success with me. I believe you have been for a whole long time. And now you have the effrontery to ask me if I'm carryin' a lot of money!

'I am carryin' money. How much is my business. I wish now I hadn't told you. In any case, I don't like the way you hang around after your brother. Like here in Eastberg. It looks to me as if you don't trust him, an' that's a fact.'

Dan's voice rose in anger. 'The only reason I asked about the money was — ' He broke off as he realised that his voice was carrying clearly beyond the alcove and that other people were getting quite an earful of a very private matter. Lowering his voice, he resumed: 'If you're carryin' a lot of money you could be in some danger, especially if you leave town.'

Della's green eyes positively flashed fire as she pushed back her chair and prepared to leave. Dan thought she looked very becoming in anger, but at the same time he knew that she was not the woman for him, nor ever had been. Millie Barre, with that hurt look in her brown eyes, compared favourably with this well-bred beautiful virago of a judge's daughter. For a moment or two, he saw the appealing image of Millie alongside of Della's angry face. The comparison pleased and calmed him.

Della moved around the table. He pushed her chair in for her. Clearly she had something further to say before she left and she was carefully picking over her words.

'Do me one small favour, for old time's sake, Dan?' she asked, with the ghost of a smile playing around the corners of her mouth.

Dan sighed. 'Yes, Della. Of course. What is it?'

'Don't offer to protect me from enemies because of the dinero I'm taking along with me, an' stay out of my way whatever happens!'

The change in the girl's expression had been sudden. She paused long enough to study Dan's reactions to her crushing words before walking out of his presence. She, in her turn, was due for a surprise.

'Della, you ain't the only pretty girl in the west. I've seen prettier. In fact I met one jest this week. So don't go thinkin' I'm wishin' myself in Vance's boots all the time. Nothin' could be further from the truth. After your recent cuttin' remarks, know that I think you're a jumped-up, over-educated, spoiled brat! But for my obligations to your father, I'd go the other way from your direction an' keep it that way for ever. It is my considered opinion that you will never grow up to be the lady the judge hoped for, an' I'm glad he's not around to hear me say so!'

Dan's last impromptu speech had the effect of making Della's knees knock. She grabbed for the back of the chair, breathing hard and apparently well beaten for the time being.

Dan put on his hat, adjusted it, nodded to her and stepped through the curtain which hid the alcove customers but allowed their words to filter through. No less than five men seated at three different tables regarded Dan with more than hostile glances.

As he stepped to the counter and paid for his food, he became aware of their hostility. Such had been his anger a short time before that it blazed forth again. He collected his change and took a few short steps towards the tables of the eavesdroppers.

Rather pointedly, he said: 'If I didn't think you were gentlemen I'd say you've been listenin' to a very private conversation concerning Judge Lacey's daughter an' that ain't considered quite the thing, even in a hick town like this one. Any of you gents got anything to say about that charge?'

No one had. Two men managed to return his hostile stare for upwards of a minute, but at length they gave in, and Dan made his way into the street still way ahead of Della. His food rumbled in his stomach. The discord over the meal had given him indigestion. He wondered what sort of a day he was going to have. A day of waiting, of frustration? Or a day of danger, with

Vance's probable duplicity underlying everything. For quite a while, as he walked the boards, Dan's spirits were low.

The fact that he had failed to eliminate any of the Vernes on the previous day had little to do with it. He was coming round to the idea that Vance was too far gone in wicked ways ever to make a decent law-abiding citizen.

And where did that leave him — Dan? A youthful former town marshal acting on a dead man's words and with little hope beyond the present protracted assignment.

*   *   *

The hours dragged by and Vance did not return. Dan took coffee with Major Hinkson in the middle of the morning, and chatted with the town marshal before lunch. When others were going indoors for their food he found that he had no appetite.

All through the hottest hours of the day he was strolling this way and that, looking for the brother who did not show up. Eventually, he found some recompense for his movements. In a large barn, situated north of the town centre, he found a familiar and welcome face. That of Millie Barre.

But first he noticed old Jerry Creel, the veteran hand from the M Bar ranch, and that gave him an inkling as to what might be happening in the rather gloomy stone building. Creel was walking up and down outside and looking troubled, especially when men's guffawing voices echoed from within.

Dan crossed over to him, asked why he was in town, and at once entered the barn. He stood at the back for a while, allowing his eyes to become accustomed to the darker interior. Millie Barre, decked out in her best clothes as if for church, was standing in front of a rickety table up on the stage appealing to the men on the benches below for ranch hands.

Seated behind the table was a fat-jowled man in a derby hat and a brown suit, who was sucking hard on a big cigar. Clearly, Millie was unaccustomed to addressing men, especially at that hour of the afternoon when they had imbibed a lot of beer. The fellow seated behind her was getting a lot of enjoyment out of her efforts to win support.

A man in the audience said: 'What makes you think that any of us here would want to work for a woman rancher, miss?'

'I don't know what makes you men tick, but a ranch is a ranch, even if the person in charge happens to be female,' Millie replied with fervour. 'So why don't you listen to me or leave the buildin'? I didn't come in here claimin' to be a polished speech-maker! All I want is help . . . Do you call yourself men?'

Anger was having its way with Millie. Already she was regretting having given up many valuable hours to ride into

Eastberg and try to drum up some worthwhile labour. She had on a green skirt and jacket. Under the jacket her lace-edged white blouse seemed small on her as she swelled it with pent-up rage. She tossed her head, swinging the brown pony's tail of hair secured at the nape of her neck.

Dan walked steadily forward down the side aisle while the fickle audience gave an angry murmur. The man with the cigar appeared to be on the side of the murmurers until Dan actually mounted to the stage and stalked across to stand beside Millie. She looked up at him without seeing for a moment, and then she gasped. He waved her into her chair, glared at the other person up there with him, and faced the audience.

'All right, so the lady asked you a question. Do you call yourselves men? Who's goin' to be the first to answer?'

About six benches were occupied. In the shadowy atmosphere many of the faces were indistinct, but clearly there was much animosity down there. After a few second's delay, a man cleared his throat and rose unsteadily to his feet.

'Now see here, stranger, I protest!'

'What did you say your name was, sir?' Dan asked ominously.

The fellow muttered to the man sitting beside him, but he declined to give his name and subsequently he slumped back on the bench. When the murmuring subsided, Dan made his move.

'If you don't like the atmosphere in here, you can leave. I reckon this young woman has hired the barn for the afternoon. All she wants is about four or five hands for her ranch, the rest of you can leave now. Unless you want to quarrel with me. In which case, stay behind.'

Dan drew his Colt from its holster, tossed it in the air, watched it somersault and caught it deftly. The man with the cigar was one of the first to leave. Others on the front bench did the same. For a few moments, it looked as if everyone was leaving.

Two men who had risen sat down again, and eventually six men stayed behind. None claimed to have any grievance with Dan, who himself assumed the task of hearing them and doing the hiring. Millie was content just to sit beside him and confirm anything that he suggested.

16

Dan had never done any hiring before. He did it well, refusing an itinerant waddy whom he had known earlier in Redrock and advising the sixth man to stick around in case any of the others failed to come up to standard.

Three men elected to go back to the ranch in a couple of hours, taking a lift on the cart with Millie and Jerry, while the others claimed to have business to wind up and insisted on going along later.

Dan partook of a light meal with the relieved young woman, who was beginning to regard him with a special look in her brown eyes which had him feeling about eight feet tall. While they were eating he intimated that if his present business worked out all right for him he would be coming to join her on the ranch in the near future.

Millie gripped his hand across the table, just as he was beginning to remember and to reflect upon the magnitude of his task and the dangers he had to face in the near future.

'Come when you can,' she murmured. 'I have some idea about what lies ahead of you. I've read the papers since we met an' the town is buzzin' with what happened yesterday an' your part in it.'

He nodded, smiled at her and promised, but she guessed at his growing restlessness.

'Is there something you have to do, in a hurry?'

'There could be, Millie. I'm keepin' watch on a certain person, an' I can't afford to be off the street for very long. I can't expect you to understand.'

Millie did, however, and they were out of doors a few minutes later. Fate, in the person of Major Hinkson, took a hand in Dan's affairs almost at once. The lawyer doffed his hat to Millie with his left hand, his other being out of action due to his recent wound and the bandaging.

'Pardon me, miss, but I have an urgent message for Dan, here. Dan, the party you conversed with earlier in the day has left town. She went in a hurry towards the west, followin' the arrival of a note brought in by a man on a wagon. I thought you might like to know.'

Dan at once became tense again. He had a feeling that for better or for worse the Mardens' dealings with the outlaws were going to be resolved. Millie could not fail to see the change in him.

'Does this mean you have to leave town at once? Do you have to follow this woman on the run?'

Dan gripped her hand, but addressed himself again to the lawyer.

'Is there any sign of my brother, Major?'

'No sign at all, Dan. I would have thought that your brother sent the message to Miss Lacey, wouldn't you?'

Hinkson sounded very surprised, and Dan felt that he had every right to be. 'I have to go after the daughter of the late Judge Lacey because I promised him I would try an' safeguard her life, Millie. I can't afford any more time, but I'll be in touch as soon as I can. Will you promise me you'll keep tryin' and be firm with those men?'

Millie did promise and at the moment of parting she brushed his cheek with her lips, oblivious to the stiff auburn side whiskers. He watched her walk away, hesitated about trying to follow her and then exchanged a few helpful words with the lawyer. Ten minutes later, he was on his way out of town towards the west.

* * *

Della Lacey drove the matched greys which had brought her from Redrock as though she was merely visiting a friend in the next valley. Dan allowed her to draw ahead. He kept up a steady pace and from time to time used his spyglass. He figured that someone had drawn her a map, and in that respect his guesswork was accurate.

Speculation eventually drove thoughts of Millie Barre to the back of his mind and he concentrated fully upon the chase and what might be waiting at the end of it. Della was driving her father's repaired buckboard and using the same team which had served the judge on the day of his death. In remembering that, Dan hoped that the Laceys would fare better on this occasion.

Within a half-hour, Della turned the vehicle off the west-bound trail into another track which was little more than a bear's route in earlier times. The wheels bounced on the new route due north, part of which was a dried-out stream bed. In time, it connected up with the regular Eastberg — Saddler's Ford trail, but soon the elusive girl had left the new track and gone off again through a meandering valley which Dan felt certain would lead eventually to Vance's hideout, the one he had once talked about with Millie.

Around half a mile separated the buckboard from the following rider when the warning shot was fired over the girl's head. The sound of the weapon's discharge echoed and reverberated all around the valley slopes, taking with it any last hope that the ride was to end in a lovers' meeting.

A hostile bullet on a jaunt of this kind was the very last thing which Della anticipated. The suddenness of it in those wide open spaces shattered her calm and made her wonder if in fact Vance was ahead of her as she had believed. A brief reflection over the pencilled message assured her that his had been the hand to write the message. She *had* to believe he was ahead of her, otherwise she was lost in every sense of the word.

Her father's untimely end swam back into her mind and she felt with great intensity the same sort of feelings he must have felt on that occasion which seemed an age ago. Panic loaned speed to the nicely matched greys. She encouraged them still further, realising how much she was likely to be dependent upon them if a chase developed.

She braced her legs against the footboard and began to look about her. On either hand were seas of prickly scrub, altogether uninviting and seemingly unpenetrable. In front there was little to give her confidence, but perhaps Vance would come to meet her. Surely fate would give her a sporting chance if she was about to be attacked by renegades?

Inevitably she began to look back over her shoulder. Her heart lurched as three riders hastily pulled out from cover on the low side of the track and began to pursue her. None of them looked familiar. Side by side they came galloping forward. They looked as if they had nothing else in mind other than overtaking her.

Too late, she remembered hints which Dan had given her that she might be in some danger clear of town with the money she was carrying. Vance had only suggested a few hundred, but she — in a rash moment — had withdrawn from the bank a similar number of thousands. At that moment, it was secreted in a flat leather case in the box underneath the seat.

In a mere few minutes, the distance between the girl and her pursuers was drastically reduced. The winding undulating trail ahead did not mean anything to her any more. Life was a matter of time, and that was fast running out. She felt sure of this when the three riders, one after another, fired a random pistol shot in her direction.

Della was sufficiently rational to realise that they were merely seeking to spook the horses at this stage, rather than shoot her.

She was turning this over in her mind when the front wheels of the conveyance fouled sprouting rocks in quick succession. The buckboard lurched first to the left and then to the right on a slight bend. Della lost her balance at the first shock. She half rose to regain it, was caught by the second vibration and precipitately tossed from her seat and away from the trail.

Her body curved away in an arc, unbidden, disappearing into a dense thicket of undergrowth on the east side. On went the horses, relieved of her weight, and the chase continued. Della was dazed and scarcely conscious when the three pursuers went through without noticing the sudden change.

The pursuit went on for over a mile before Long John himself discovered that the girl was missing. He showed surprise which was scarcely minimised when his brothers discovered that the box from under the seat had also been ripped from its moorings before they caught up.

17

Purely by chance, Long John, Jake and Little Sam failed to notice the lone rider who was tailing the girl on the buckboard. Dan, on the other hand, had a revealing glimpse of his three old enemies as they came out of cover and took up the chase. His earlier forebodings now seemed to be giving way to reality.

As the ex-town marshal shook his big dun horse into a new and faster rhythm, he knew that the late judge's only daughter was up ahead of him and in dire trouble from the men who had killed her father. He remembered all too clearly the judge's dying words and he knew that he had to take chances, more chances than at any other time, otherwise Della Lacey, the last of the Laceys, did not have long to live.

The men who were pursuing her

were not the kind to leave her unmolested on account of her being a female. They hated everything to do with the judge and it was doubtful if she would live to converse with anyone else, unless they took pleasure in torturing her.

The flurry of shooting aimed at upsetting the greys kept Dan informed of the progress up ahead. He pulled his own gun and tried to decide when he should fire it in order to distract the trio before they actually caught up with the girl. He had topped a rise and was almost on the point of firing his gun when something sparkling, reflecting the sun's rays, attracted him from a shurb on the low side.

Instinct made him slow down and investigate further. Next, he saw what it was. A womans long hat pin with a red cut stone on the end of it. The one Della sometimes wore in her riding hat to keep it in place over her hair. Moreover, the hat pin was still sticking in the cloth of the pale grey flat-topped stetson.

The broken twigs in evidence and a faint sound which could easily be interpreted as the cry of a woman in some pain or fear made Dan think that Della was somewhere in the thicket close by. He called to her and she answered in an animated whisper.

'I'm almost torn to bits with thorn. My elbows are skinned and one of my knees is swelling, but I don't think I have any broken bones. Do come an' try to release me, Dan. I'm sorry about everything I said earlier.'

'Keep your voice down. I'm coming. There has to be a place to hide the dun before your buddies, the Vernes, get back again.'

Some thirty yards further on Dan succeeded in finding a way through the thick undergrowth and presently he came upon Della's prostrate form under the lower branches of two stunted trees which had almost succumbed to the encroaching growth around them.

Below her position was a shallow hollow. Dan directed her into it and entreated her not to talk.

★　★　★

The Vernes came back still in their formation of three. They had no reason to suppose that a crouching gunman was only willing them closer to his weapons, and their full attention was given over to searching the ground on either side of the track for the missing girl.

Fifty yards away, they slowed and John pointed up the slope to where the accident had happened. 'For my money, she left the buckboard up there an' we have to look for her on the east side. So let's start lookin'.'

Up they came, slowing a little and fidgeting with their weapons. Dan was glad of that because he had no intention whatever of giving them any warning of his presence. He reminded himself of the sort of errand they were on, and how they had treated the judge. These thoughts were all he needed to stiffen his resolve.

The upper trunks of all three were reasonably silhouetted against nature's background as they slowly jogged up the slope nicely within shooting distance for Dan's Winchester. He debated with himself for nearly a minute before selecting Long John, the most deadly of the three, as his primary victim.

Little Sam was on the far side of him and Jake's stockingfoot roan was fine-stepping on the near side. Dan saw them so clearly that it all seemed unreal. Just as he was about to pull the trigger of his Winchester, John suddenly pointed his right-hand revolver. The action was disconcerting but he was only practising. This far, he had seen nothing to add credence to his earlier theorising.

Dan lined him up again. The squeezing of the trigger was a long, fine-drawn effort. Long John threw back his head, as though reacting to the buffeting sounds of the gunshot. The outlaw leader appeared to stiffen, and then he went backwards over his horse's tail.

The other two had accepted the warning. Sam went to one side and Jake hauled the stockingfoot to the other. Dan hastily lined up on Jake and fired as the roan hurled itself forward. His second bullet must have missed by no more than an inch, but a miss was a miss.

Jake's bullets, fired from a revolver, started to spray the ground around Dan's position. Gritting his teeth, the ambusher ignored the danger and instead panned his weapon in the direction of the third man. Little Sam, who could move very swiftly when he felt the need to do so, put his bay gelding head first into the foliage on his own side of the track, regardless of the hazards. The gelding whinnied with fright but went on, and the rider was partially hidden by the foliage of stunted trees by the time the hostile

Winchester sounded off again.

Mindful that he might have failed with his third target, Dan fired no less than three shots into the spot where horse and man had disappeared and, in doing so, he missed a further chance against Jake, who took the opportunity to collect his armoury and dive into cover on the nearer, more vulnerable side.

The echoes faded away. Long John's black stallion had turned about and retreated. Jake's stockingfoot made a spirited run, only to swing away to the side and go into timber rather farther away than its master. Significantly, Sam's gelding did not reappear.

In spite of the element of surprise, Dan did not think that he had done particularly well in the opening exchanges of what promised to be a battle to the death.

The cat-and-mouse between Jake and Dan developed slowly, and not before Della had called out in a half-strangled voice to know if all was going well.

Perspiration had spread in a patch across the shoulders of Dan's shirt. Further beads trickled slowly down his sideburns. He shifted his position a little, so that he faced towards the direction in which Jake had gone to earth.

There were, perhaps, three hours of daylight left. One of them slipped by like an age. Dan's eyes played tricks. The only hint he had as to the progress which Jake was making came when the outlaw went rather close to the spot where the dun was cropping yellowed grass. The animal made a noise recognisable to Dan and gave him something to go on. Even so, when he had shifted his position another ten yards and made adjustments to his direction, Jake almost deceived him.

Della could see the outlaw in the closing stages of his advance. Holding her breath so as not to draw a bullet in her own direction, she lifted a stone about the size of her fist and tossed it through the air in the direction of the tree behind which Jake was hidden.

The stone actually struck the bole at the very moment when Jake sprang clear with his rifle to his shoulder. Startled by the noise, Dan rolled over. While his body was still turning on the earth he sighted Jake and fired off two bullets with his Winchester only partially controlled. And then he was rolling over again.

Jake got off one shot as a bullet hit him high in the chest and sent him backwards. Dan was to remember the ludicrous turn of expression on the killer's lined face for many a long year. Jake, the thick-waisted fellow in the round black stetson, died as his body closed with the earth.

For a short while Dan stood over him, willing his breathing to ease and hearing the heart-rending sobbing of the girl who had saved him by her brave effort. Five minutes later, after reloading and checking that the girl was unhurt, Dan broke cautiously from cover and went in search of Little Sam, the member of the gang he felt he knew best.

He was steeling himself for another long unpleasant game of cat-and-mouse on the lower slope when the unexpected happened.

'Hey, is that you, Marden?'

The voice came from much lower down the slope than Dan had anticipated. It belonged to Little Sam, but it sounded ragged. Dan guessed that he had been hurt. Of the bay there was no sign. Dan kept quite still and waited for another call. Unknown to him, he almost waited in vain.

'Hey, you up there!'

This time the shout occasioned some painful coughing and Dan felt justified in his thinking that Sam was hurt. He began to move down the slope, assuming that the big outlaw had either fallen heavily or absorbed one of the bullets fired into the trees after him.

Dan was right in both his assumptions. During the latter stages of the exchanges between Dan and Jake, Sam had lost a lot of blood from a wound in his abdomen. It was one of those wounds which almost always resulted in death in his day and age. Sam had tried to make his own way down to a small stream which trickled along the perimeter of the timber stand into which he had escaped.

Unfortunately the drain on his blood had considerably weakened him. He now knew that he would not make it to the water. He preferred to meet again with his enemy rather than die without having seen another mortal.

Dan overtook him when he was near the end. Sam had gone without his weapons. This phenomenon did much to convince Dan that his enemy had not long to live.

'You're the last of the trio, Sam. Why did you all take off after the judge's daughter like that? I've known you do more manly things.'

Sam grinned with an effort, but his hirsute face still looked drained and all the colour in his body seemed to have gone into the blood seeping from his broken lips.

'Money, Marden, what else? Money.' Sam's eyes flickered.

Thinking that Sam was on the point of death, Dan unslung the water canteen which he had brought with him and advanced to give the outlaw a drink. Miraculously, the dying man recovered. His face, due to the awkward position into which he had fallen, was upside down to Dan. Nevertheless, Sam contrived to make his wants known.

'Toss it down,' he instructed. 'I'll get it if I need it.'

Dan respected his last wish and leaned against a tree bole, wondering if he knew all he needed to know about these killers on the trails and their associations with his brother. Sam responded almost as though he could read thoughts.

'You'll find Vance all right, but he won't be to your likin'. John finally ran out of patience with him. You'll see, town marshal. The Vernes have taken a lot of jaspers with them, includin' a famous judge an' your brother.'

Dan heard and saw everything in Sam Verne's dying minutes, but he remained stock-still beside the tree which supported him, feeling with a deep inner conviction that he was hearing the truth about Vance. He realised that unconsciously he had not expected Vance to survive.

* * *

Della came limping down the slope some five minutes later. She had recovered her hat and a little bit of her poise, but the brightness of her eyes showed that her nerves were on edge and that she was in no state to be left on her own.

'I have to thank you for savin' my life, Dan,' she began.

Dan nodded. 'I was actin' for your Pa, an' you did your share, in any case. Right now, we have things to do. I want to locate Vance before sunset. And what's more, I think I ought to warn you that Little Sam said my brother was dead. If you want to take your buck-board an' clear off back into town, I'll understand.'

Della absorbed the stupefying news with a few vestiges of dignity. She bathed her wounds down by the stream and insisted in helping with pressing chores before they could be on their way. Dan was workmanlike and thorough. He rounded up all the spare horses and used them to carry the corpses to the buckboard.

While he was doing so, Della had the good fortune to find the satchel containing the missing money. She stowed it and the box it had travelled in back under the seat of the buckboard and pronounced herself quite capable of driving the two greys on the rest of the journey.

Some forty minutes later the terrain changed again. Dan already had an inkling that they were nearing their journey's end. He became sure when the same thoroughbred palomino horse which he had seen in Eastberg suddenly appeared on the edge of timber and whinnied a welcome to the other quadrupeds.

The log shack in the tree-shadowed valley had the benefit of a narrow stream and was improved by many wild flowers of varying colours. The two newcomers, however, had no eyes for nature's natural beauty. Della dropped behind while Dan pressed forward with a gun in his hand, determined not to be defeated by any form of last-minute treachery.

The man who had built the shack was good with tools. His home-made table, chairs and bunks bore witness to that. The place was absolutely quiet, except for the minute noises of a few flies which would give more of their attention to the sad familiar drooping figure which in death had laid its stetsoned head on the smooth surface of the table. Vance had died a few hours earlier. A knife had been thrown at him from the doorway, hurled by an expert who had hit him in the chest and severed an important blood vessel.

He had been left to die. In the short time left to him, he had extracted the knife and used it to leave a last message. With the point of the death weapon he had scratched words on the table top.

I tried to play straight with you D . . .

Life had failed him as he struggled to make Dan's name, knowing he would come. The knife was still clutched in his right hand. The right arm hung over the end of the table, drooping towards the floor. Della saw the sad tableau and wilted. Whisky brought her round and later she was able to light the stove and make a meal.

That night, Vance lay in state under a blanket on the table. Della slept in the loft. The Vernes spent the night under a tarpaulin around the back of the cabin, while Dan slept alone beside a fire not far from the door.

Sleep was slow in coming, and yet he

was not troubled by the lack of it. He found his mind going back to earlier days when Vance and he were boys; before the civil war claimed their respected father and while their mother was still a young and pretty woman.

From time to time, he found himself whistling songs which their mother had taught them at the piano and wondering what had happened to the Jew's-harp which his father took away to the wars. Although he did not realise it, he was taking part in a lone lament for his brother.

When his eyelids started to grow heavy he made a cigarette out of the last of his tobacco and gazed into the fire. Ahead of him there was a lot of digging, burying, escorting and explaining to do, but he had come through to the end of this bitter life-taking assignment which had started with the sudden death of the old judge and ended with the sad demise of Vance in his prime.

After Eastberg, his future lay with a

warm-hearted brown-eyed lonesome rancher's daughter who could give him all the work he needed to make him forget the passing of his only kin.

THE END

We do hope that you have enjoyed reading this large print book.

Did you know that all of our titles are available for purchase?

We publish a wide range of high quality large print books including:
Romances, Mysteries, Classics
General Fiction
Non Fiction and Westerns

Special interest titles available in large print are:
The Little Oxford Dictionary
Music Book, Song Book
Hymn Book, Service Book

Also available from us courtesy of Oxford University Press:
Young Readers' Dictionary
(large print edition)
Young Readers' Thesaurus
(large print edition)

For further information or a free brochure, please contact us at:
Ulverscroft Large Print Books Ltd.,
The Green, Bradgate Road, Anstey,
Leicester, LE7 7FU, England.
Tel: (00 44) **0116 236 4325**
Fax: (00 44) **0116 234 0205**

*Other titles in the
Linford Western Library:*

RAOUL'S TREASURE

Skeeter Dodds

Arriving in Bradley Creek, Jack Strother defends an old man and is pitched into a confrontation with Ben Bradley, the region's biggest rancher. Now an enemy of Bradley, Strother leaves town, but is forced to return on learning that the old man is dying and wishes to pass on something. But what he gives Strother leads him to a mountain of trouble near the Mexican border. Will the future be no more than a grave in the desert?